MACMILLAN CHILDREN'S BOOKS

THE REAL FAMILY CHRISTMAS

Sue Mongredien

ILLUSTRATED BY

Kate Pankhurst

First published 2019 by Macmillan Children's Books
an imprint of Pan Macmillan
The Smithson, 6 Briset Street, London EC1M 5NR
Associated companies throughout the world
www.panmacmillan.com

ISBN 978-1-5290-0693-3

1 3 5 7 9 8 6 4 2

A CIP catalogue record for this book is available from
the British Library.

Printed and bound by CPI Group (UK) Ltd, Croydon CR0 4YY

MIX
Paper from
responsible sources
FSC® C116313

UNCLE
CHRISTMAS

CHAPTER ONE

Many years ago, **Father Christmas** was a young man and looked very different. His beard was brown and tufty. His tummy was quite a lot smaller. He had sparkly eyes and a big friendly smile, but he looked tired and rather worried, because this was his first year in the job. He was working very hard making toys and presents for good children everywhere and really wanted to make Christmas a brilliant success.

His younger brother, **Harry Christmas**, was *not* such a hard worker. Harry spent his days

having snowball fights with the elves, going for long gallops on the reindeer and thinking up new pranks.

Unfortunately, the pranks often went wrong.

SMASH! He didn't *mean* to break the workshop window with that snowball!

CRASH! He didn't even notice the sleigh was *there*!

WHOOPS! The icicle was supposed to slither down his brother's *jumper*, not jab him on the nose!

Now Father Christmas – or *Nick*, as his

family called him – was very kind and loved his brother, but as November slid into December and the winter winds blew colder, time was running out to get everything ready for Christmas Eve. He was busier than ever, thanks to all the hopeful letters from children that had come pouring in from all around the world.

Dear Father Christmas, I would really like a toy car and a new football, please.
Love Tommy Woodgrove

Dear Father Christmas, I'll be so happy if you bring me some ice skates! Thank you!
From Freya Gudrunsdottir

Dear Father Christmas, Please can I have some new crayons and a book?
Love Chibunda Adebayo

And so it went on. 'The problem is, I know some of these children have been quite naughty recently,' Nick said over breakfast with a frown. He and Harry were at home in their cosy cottage near the North Pole. A log fire crackled in the grate as snowflakes pattered softly against the windows.

Nick dipped a soldier of toast into his boiled egg and held up another letter. 'Here – Ling Wu, for example. According to the Tinselnet, she was rude to her teacher at school *three times* last month *and* pretended she had lost her homework. As for Jack Morris – just last week he was feeding his broccoli under the table to the dog, when he told his dad he had eaten it all himself!

Harry gave a shrug. Moments earlier, he had actually been sneaking his toast crusts to **Wolfie**, their own dog, under the table, and couldn't see the big deal.

'I bet Jack's dog was pleased,' he pointed out. 'As for Ling Wu's homework,' he went on, 'doesn't *everyone* do that sort of thing?' He was pretty sure he'd invented lots of unlikely reasons for not finishing homework himself back in his school days, after all.

'No!' cried Nick. '**Good children** don't.' He read another letter and spluttered crossly.

'And here's Anya Abalov asking for a new bike . . .

when I know for a fact that she thinks it's funny to sit on her younger brother and fart on him. I mean, honestly! Does she *deserve* a present?'

Harry chuckled. 'You've got to admit, that *is* quite funny,' he said. 'Not for the younger brother, obviously,' he added, in case Nick got any ideas about doing it to *him*. 'But you can't leave her off your present list, just because of that. **Naughty people can still be *nice*!**'

Nick got to his feet, brushing crumbs from his beard. 'At this rate, there won't be enough presents anyway,' he said glumly, glancing at his watch. 'I'd better head to the workshop and crack on. I've got six thousand, seven hundred and ninety-three toys to finish today if I'm going to hit my target.'

Harry's eyebrows shot up. That was a *lot* of toys. When their dad had been Father Christmas, the elves had always helped him make presents for the **Big Night**. But ever since Nick had taken charge of the workshop that year, he had laid down some strict new rules.

No *singing!*
No *joke-telling!*
No *laughing or flicking sawdust at each other or being silly!*

It was all because he was worried about not getting the toys made in time, but one by one, the elves had become fed up and left. Even Harry had been banned from helping after he dropped twenty-seven jigsaw puzzles and all the pieces got muddled up. But it hadn't been **on purpose!**

'Look, if you change your mind about wanting another pair of hands—' he began.

Nick shook his head. 'I can manage,'

he replied, like he always did.

Harry went back to his breakfast. He thought his big brother was great most of the time, but every now and then, he did make Harry feel a bit . . . well, a bit *useless*. As if he wasn't clever enough to join in with the really important Christmassy stuff.

'Okay,' he mumbled in reply.

'Actually, there *is* something you could do,' Nick said as he reached the doorway, and Harry brightened. 'Look, I hate to mention it again but it's your turn to **wash up**. Do you think you might be able to do it today?'

Harry glanced guiltily over at the sink where there were towers of pots and pans, a mountain of plates, and a whole army of dirty mugs clustered together. **Oops**. He had been meaning to get around to that.

'Sure, absolutely,' he replied, then buttered another piece of toast and decided to see how much jam he could blob on top. Quite a lot actually. *WIBBLE! WOBBLE!* Whoa! Almost half the jar was on his toast now. 'Hey, look!' he laughed, holding the heavy slice up to show his brother. But Nick had already gone.

Harry rolled his eyes and took a bite. That brother of his worked too hard! Why couldn't he be more like Harry, and just enjoy life?

*

The beginning of December became the middle of December, and then, suddenly

Harry's advent calendar was up to the 20th of December, and Christmas itself was just around the corner. Only a few days were left until the sleigh had to be loaded up with presents, the reindeer harnessed and their hooves dusted with **special *flying* magic!** Before any of that could happen though, Nick still had to finish making thousands of presents, and wrap them all up.

He was working so hard now he barely had time to sleep. Even worse, he had caught a cold. A ***snotty, sneezy, wheezy*** cold with a burning head, a scratchy throat and a sore shiny nose.

'I dobe feeb vebby webb,' he confessed over breakfast that morning, blowing his nose for the sixty-seventh time.

'What's that, bro?' asked Harry, only half listening. He'd gone off for a gallop with Blitzen, his favourite reindeer, the day before and they'd come across the most *amazing* ice slide on the other side of the forest. It had been so much fun! He definitely needed to tell the elves about it today, so they could have fun whizzing down it too.

'Godda code,' sniffled Nick before an enormous sneeze exploded from his nostrils.

WAAAAH-*CHOO!*

He dabbed at his nose and shuffled towards the door. Then he stopped and sighed as he noticed the sink which was **full** of dirty dishes again. 'Um. Harry,' he said before a coughing fit took over his voice.

'Yep, yep, washing-up, okay,' Harry replied distractedly. 'I'm going to tackle it, don't worry. Any day now.' His thoughts returned to the ice slide and how fast he had *zoomed* around its corners. It had almost felt like flying! 'Hey, I don't suppose you fancy coming to try the **ice slide** I found, do you?' he asked, turning towards his brother. But Nick had already hurried off to work.

Harry's toast was cold so he gave it to Wolfie then headed out to meet his elf pals. They would definitely be up for some sliding, at least. Elves loved being busy and ever since they'd stopped working for Nick, they'd often grumbled about having nothing to do up here in the frozen north. **Bring on the fun!** he thought cheerfully.

*

Soon they were all setting off towards the ice slide: Harry and Wolfie, Ginger and Juniper, Candy and . . . oh, almost *all* of the elves, in fact. Only Biff, who was getting on a bit and preferred a quieter life, chose to stay at home with his knitting.

Snow was falling in big wet flakes as they reached the edge of the forest, and their boots made *creaking* sounds as they tramped along excitedly. The forest was still and quiet apart from a few scampering squirrels who watched them with beady eyes. Wolfie, whose favourite thing in the whole world was chasing squirrels, sniffed the air enthusiastically and galloped ahead.

'Here we are,' said Harry, when they arrived. 'What do you think?'

The elves' faces lit up as they saw the long, twisting slide. What did they *think*? **They all *loved* it!** So much so that in the next second, all of them were jostling to be first, throwing themselves on to the slippery surface and squealing excitedly as they whizzed down, one after another.

ZOOM! ZOOM! ZOOM!

'Wheeeeee!'

'Woohoo!'

'Wahey!'

'Whoop-dee-doo!'

It was the best fun any of them had had all year. Soon the whole valley was filled with the sounds of laughter and happy shrieks. As he shot down the slide with his friends, Harry couldn't help wishing that Nick could be there with them, to enjoy it too. But just as he was thinking this, there came a shout, and Harry turned to see Biff, puffing and panting as he jogged through the snow towards them.

'*Biff!*' cried Harry as the old elf reached the clearing and bent over to catch his breath. **'Is everything okay?'**

'It's Father Christmas,' wheezed Biff, red in the face with sweat popping out on his nose.

'He's collapsed!'

CHAPTER TWO

Harry and the elves *raced* home to find Nick grey in the face and very poorly looking. After helping him into bed, Harry called for the **Flying Doctors** and asked them to come out as soon as possible. Because the Christmas family lived so far from other people, it often took a while for visitors to reach them, but thankfully a helicopter landed before long, and out stepped a kind-faced doctor, who introduced herself as Annie.

'Oh dear,' she said, when she took Nick's temperature. 'The thermometer says *Boiling Boiling Hot*. I'm afraid you've got the flu. Keep nice and warm in bed for a few days, drink plenty of broth and cold drinks, and above all, have a jolly good rest,' she said, putting the thermometer back in her bag.

'**Impossible**,' croaked Nick. 'I'm Father Christmas. I'm far too busy to rest.'

Doctor Annie's blue eyes went very big and round when she heard this. 'You're . . . you're Father Christmas?' she gasped. 'Oh my goodness. Thank you for all of my presents! That scooter with flashing wheels you gave me when I was ten was, like, the *best thing ever*!' Then she frowned and put her head on one side.

'Wait though,' she said. 'You can't be Father Christmas – surely you're not old enough!'

Nick smiled bashfully. 'Well . . .' he said before sneezing into his handkerchief.

Harry took over the explanation. 'The scooter must have been from our dad,' he told Annie. 'He was Father Christmas before Nick here, and our grandpa before that. The eldest son takes on the job whenever the old Father Christmas retires – and Dad hung up his red coat and hat on Boxing Day last year. His eyesight got quite bad – he didn't feel safe driving the sleigh any more.'

'Oh my,' said Annie, blinking as if she was trying to take this all in. 'So this is your **first year** as Father Christmas?'

Nick nodded rather glumly.

Then Annie looked back at Harry. 'And so you must be . . . what, *Uncle* **Christmas?**' she asked him.

Harry shrugged. 'I guess,' he replied. 'But you can call me Harry.'

'And you can call me Nick,' said Nick, blowing his poor red nose.

'Well, Nick, however busy you might be, you'll have to **take it easy** for a while,' Annie told him. 'Doctor's orders. Harry – you need to look after your brother for the next few days. Understood?'

Harry and Nick exchanged a worried glance. 'But . . .' said Nick, who had been looking forward to his first **Big Night** as Father Christmas all year.

'The thing is . . .' said Harry, who had never been in charge of anything in his life.

'Good,' said Annie before they could argue. She closed her doctor's bag with a snap and got to her feet. 'Ring the Flying Doctors if you start feeling any worse, and one of us will come back to check up on you. I'll see myself out.'

Nick shut his eyes and fell limply back against the pillow. Harry hesitated, wondering what to do. *Surely* his brother would be back on his feet in time to make the deliveries on Christmas Eve? He had to be!

Outside there came the sound of the helicopter's engine starting up, its rotor blades turning faster and faster. **CHOP!** **CHOP!** **CHOP!** **CHOP-*CHOP*-CHOP!**

CHOPCHOPCHOP! Then, through the window, Harry saw the helicopter taking off and flying away into the big snowy sky. All of a sudden, he felt very alone.

He gulped as he thought about all the children around the world who were looking forward to Christmas Eve, who had written letters asking for special presents and were counting down the days. **It was kind of terrifying**. He bit his lip and told himself that his brother just had a teeny-weeny cold and would wake up soon feeling completely well again. Probably in an hour or so. Of course he would!

*

As Harry quietly shut Nick's bedroom door and went downstairs, he couldn't help noticing how *messy* the house had become lately. Dust speckled the surfaces and cobwebs dangled from corners. Sofa cushions were still scattered across the living-room floor from where some of the elves had come round to watch Christmas films the other evening. With Nick ill in bed, it was up to Harry now to do everything, and the thought was pretty alarming. *Older* brothers were meant to be in charge, not younger ones! How was he going to manage on his own?

Just then there was a **whistling** sound in the chimney and a huge pile of envelopes came thumping down into the fireplace. *WHEEEE . . . BUMPITY-BUMP!* More letters from children, Harry guessed, all excitedly asking for the toys and presents they most wanted to be given for Christmas.

It was impossible, it really was. If he and Nick couldn't make this Christmas as fun and happy as all the ones before, they would be letting everyone down!

Wait though, he thought, eyes narrowing as he went over to the heap of mail. What was that on the top? He picked up a postcard showing a gorgeous beach scene with palm trees and white sand. Flipping it over, he saw his mum's handwriting on the other side.

Dear boys,

Having a lovely time here in Honolulu. Your dad's taken up surfing and I've had a go at scuba diving. Great fun! Just wanted

to wish you all the best for a successful
Christmas Eve this year – I'm sure you're all
set! Enjoy the magic. We'll keep an eye out
for the sleigh and give you a wave!
Love Mum and Dad xxx

Harry and Nick's parents had been on holiday
ever since they retired from Christmas duties. 'You
get to travel the world, being Father Christmas,
but **only in the *dark*,**' his dad had said when
they'd first planned the adventure. 'Now I'd like
to visit everywhere again, by daylight, and take
my time about it. And be with your mother!'

Harry propped the postcard up on the
mantelpiece – then had a brilliant idea. **Yes!**
That was it! His dad was an expert at being
Father Christmas and his mum was a skilled

toymaker and present-wrapper. Who better to ask for help? They wouldn't mind popping back for a few days to muck in, would they? Of course not!

He smiled with relief as he rushed to the phone and dialled. 'Mum, hi, it's Harry,' he said, when she picked up. He could hear the sound of waves crashing in the distance, and music playing – then a roar of applause and cheering. 'Hello?'

'Hi, darling! Lovely to hear from you!' cried his mum. Then he heard her laughing. '*Woohoo!* Well done, love! That was amazing!'

'Mum?' asked Harry, frowning.

'Sorry, your dad was just taking part in the island *limbo-dancing* competition. Ooh, they're

popping
such a pretty
garland of
flowers on
his head right
now. What a

picture he looks!' Her laughter tinkled down

the phone. 'So how are you boys? All set? I'm

surprised you've got time to chat right now, when

it's getting so close to the **Big Night!**'

'Yeah,' said Harry. 'Well, actually, that's why

I'm calling. We're not *quite* "all set" because

Nick's ill. He's got the flu so . . .'

'Oh goodness,' his mum interrupted,

sounding excited. 'So *you're* stepping in this

year instead? **Oh, *Harry!*** I always hoped that

31

would happen! I know it's been hard, being the younger brother with Nick getting the glory of the job, and – well, not that I'd *want* your brother to be ill obviously, the poor lamb, but I'm **thrilled** you'll have a chance to put on the red suit and head off on the sleigh instead. Wait till I tell your dad!'

Harry grimaced, looking around at the messy room and all the unopened letters by his feet. 'The thing is though, we're . . . a bit behind,' he confessed. 'So I was wondering—'

'Oh, the elves will step it up a gear for the big finale, don't worry,' she replied breezily. 'They're such hard workers, they really pull out all the stops. We had a few **tricky** years too, when you boys were tiny and there was so much to do, but it always worked out in the end. And honestly, you'll have the **best night of your life** on Christmas Eve, you really will!'

'But Mum—' Harry put in. The conversation wasn't exactly going the way he'd planned. He could hardly tell her that the elves hadn't been in the workshop since Nick upset them with his new rules.

'What an honour, darling! Listen, I'd better go, it's my turn in the limbo dancing. But we'll be thinking of you on Christmas Eve! Have a wonderful time! **We believe in you!**'

And then there was a click, and she'd hung up. Harry sank down into the sofa, knowing that he absolutely couldn't ring back and ask for help. Not when his parents were having such a lovely holiday and his mum had sounded so happy for him.

Wolfie ambled over and Harry scratched him behind the ears. 'We'll just have to make the best of it ourselves, mate,' he said worriedly. 'Somehow. Otherwise Christmas is going to be ruined . . . and **it will all be my fault!**'

CHAPTER THREE

Harry cleaned the kitchen until everything gleamed, then made his brother some soup and a cup of tea, and took it in to him on a tray. Nick was drowsy and his forehead still burned to the touch, but he mumbled his thanks before his eyes flickered shut again.

After that, Harry sat down in front of the **Tinselnet**, which kept a running list of the children who deserved gifts in their stockings. Harry knew Nick had already made *thousands* of presents in the workshop, but how many *more* would be needed? Time to find out.

Clicking a button to refresh the screen, two numbers appeared under the headings **Nice** and **Naughty**. To Harry's surprise though, the number beneath "Nice" was dropping every minute, whereas the number beneath "Naughty" kept going up at the same rate. That was strange. Was there some naughtiness epidemic breaking out across the world? Or was the Tinselnet getting muddled up somehow?

He clicked on the **Naughty** column and saw name after name appearing, with the reason for their inclusion.

Alfonso Lopez –

sneaking into his parents' room to see if he could spot any presents

Maarika Bunyasarn –
nibbling the corner of a gingerbread decoration

Ninsei Komura –
refusing to come down to dinner

Harry pulled a face. The Tinselnet was being very harsh, he thought. Sneaking around looking for presents and nibbling gingerbread because you were so excited about Christmas . . . these weren't **bad** things! It didn't mean the children were *naughty*! As for not wanting to come down to dinner . . . Harry clicked on the boy's name and a small video screen came up, of Ninsei Komura lying on his bedroom floor, colouring a beautiful card for his family.

'He's being *nice*!' Harry told the machine crossly. 'He's trying to finish this lovely card, that's all. Why are you being so mean?'

A thought occurred to him, and he clicked on the "Settings" button. The screen changed and Harry peered closer. Ah – so that was why the Tinselnet was judging all these excited children so severely, he realized. Because someone had turned the behaviour setting all the way up to **"Really *Really* Strict"**.

When Father Christmas was meant to be the kindest, most loving person in the world!

Harry shook his head in exasperation. Nick had always been good as a boy, so he'd never understood that an occasional bit of naughtiness didn't make someone a bad person! It certainly shouldn't mean they didn't deserve any presents.

With a quick glance over his shoulder to check he wasn't being watched, Harry changed the Tinselnet setting down past "**Strict**" to "**Not Really Very Strict At All**" and then all the way down to "**Hey, It's *Christmas*, Everyone Makes Mistakes Once In A While**". There, that was more like it, he thought, pressing "Save". Everybody deserved to be happy at Christmas. And Harry was going to do his best to make sure they were.

Unfortunately though, when he went back to the main screen he saw that the "**Naughty**" column now had a big fat zero underneath it . . . and that the number beneath the "**Nice**" column was . . . quite a lot bigger. Harry gulped, rubbed his eyes and checked the figure again. Still as massive as before. He was really going to need a *lot* of help making the rest of the toys if all of those children were going to wake up on Christmas morning with a present or two. And if he wanted the elves to come back to the workshop, then maybe it was time he changed Nick's strict rules. What his brother didn't know about wouldn't hurt him, right?

He hurried out towards the elves' houses. '**Is anyone free to lend me a hand, please?**' he called out, knocking on door after door. 'Your brilliant toy-making skills are needed like never before. And you can *sing* and have as much fun as you like, I promise!'

*

As soon as the elves found out that Nick wasn't there to boss them around or get cross with them, **great excitement** broke out. With much giggling and squealing, they burst into the Christmas workshop, put on their special aprons and wasted no time in getting things exactly how they liked them.

Candy and Ginger set about making *delicious* sweets and treats in one corner and the air soon filled with the smells of cinnamon, vanilla and chocolate.

Juniper and Perky led a team making wooden toys, and the workshop buzzed with the sounds of sawing and sanding.

Holly and Tinsel organized the wrapping and

decoration group, while Pine and Peppermint dusted off the sewing machines and set about the cuddly-toy production line. Biff, looking rather bashful, appeared with a whole **sackful** of children's scarves and gloves he'd been knitting all year, just in case. 'I do like keeping busy,' he explained.

Meanwhile Rudy and Elvis joined Harry in checking through all the presents that Nick had made so far. There were **piles** of beautifully carved chess sets, a teetering tower of solitaire games, boxes and boxes of jigsaw puzzles and hundreds of quiz books. Harry picked up a wooden block puzzle and examined it. Everything had been nicely made, and Nick had obviously worked extremely hard, but . . .

'Listen, **I don't want to be rude**,' Rudy said just then.

'. . . But these are kind of *boring* toys,' Elvis finished.

Harry knew what they meant. Nick had been so sensible and clever growing up that these were the sorts of toys he'd loved most as a boy. Harry, on the other hand, had always preferred kicking a ball or throwing a Frisbee, toys that made funny noises, or games that were loud and silly. Children were *different* – and they liked different things! Not **everyone** wanted to sit still for hours, carefully completing a jigsaw.

'Okay, so while these are all great, we do need a good mixture of presents,' he said aloud. 'Ice skates and balls for kids who like to be active,' he went on, remembering some of the letters that had come in earlier that month. 'Art sets for children who love drawing,' he added, thinking about Ninsei Komura's neat colouring. 'Magic tricks and ping-pong bats . . .'

'Dolls and teddies and fluffy **unicorns**,' added Rudy.

'Toy castles and train sets and those *really cool* walkie-talkies,' suggested Elvis.

'Yes, to all of those,' Harry agreed. 'Everything that children have been asking for in their letters, in fact! But **do we have time** to make so many new toys, do you think?'

'Absolutely!' cried Rudy, rolling up his sleeves.

'It's what we love doing **best**!' agreed Elvis

happily, before bustling away to instruct a team of helpers.

Harry looked around at the busy workshop, smiling as some of the elves started singing a Christmas song together in one corner. This was more like it! The elves belonged here: they were cheerful hard workers, they all had amazing ideas for presents and what was more, they loved making them.

'**Thank you, everyone**,' he called out gratefully, throwing on an apron and going to help Nutmeg and Merry who were constructing awesome-looking water pistols. 'You're all stars. We can do this!'

*

The next few days passed in a whirl. Harry

and the elves worked long hours making and wrapping toys and treats but it was much more **fun** than Harry had expected. Every now and then Cherry and Pip would appear with trays of freshly baked cinnamon buns or gingerbread, everyone sang **jolly Christmas songs** to keep up their spirits and the workshop was cosy and warm while the snow fell thickly outside. Even Wolfie had been busy, testing out the new footballs, and dusting the cobwebs off the sleigh with his big waggy tail. Okay, so he also managed to get tangled up in tinsel at one point, and made quite a few of the cinnamon buns 'disappear' but he was doing his best.

'Good dog,' Harry said approvingly, scratching behind his shaggy ears.

Nick, meanwhile, was still poorly. He coughed all night. His nose was red and runny. His temperature had gone down a tiny weeny bit but still showed as *Boiling Hot* on the thermometer.

'**Stay in bed until next week** – doctor's orders,' said Annie when she popped in to visit. 'Nice job with the cleaning by the way,' she added approvingly, winking at Harry.

Harry couldn't help a tingle of pride. He had never worked harder, or felt more tired in his life – but he was *happy* too. It was so satisfying to see the piles of presents building up ready to be delivered – presents that he himself had helped make!

As well as the pride though, he couldn't help feeling a twist of guilt that he hadn't done more to help Nick before now. They could have been a team, along with the elves, and then they'd have been ready for the **Big Night** in plenty of time. Harry should have made more of an effort to get involved instead of mucking about so much, he thought glumly.

Still, at least he had made up for it now, he reasoned. In fact, maybe after all this, Nick would realize that Harry *was* a hard worker, and *was* responsible, **not just a silly kid brother** who mucked things up all the time. It could happen, right?

*

By the time a fat red sun was sinking low in the sky on Christmas Eve, Harry was starting to think that he and the elves might *just* have done enough to rescue Christmas. The final present had been made, along with a few spares for good measure, and now the elves were hastily wrapping the last batch so they'd be ready to load up into the sleigh. The reindeers' coats had been brushed, and they'd eaten a big dinner of hot oats and carrots ready for their long journey. Before Harry put on the famous red trousers, jacket and hat and set off into the night, all he had left to do was to **rub the magic *flying* dust** into the reindeers' hooves.

Harry went into the stable and patted Rudolph's long velvety nose. 'Can you believe it? We're almost ready to go. This is actually happening – and I'm really and truly **going to be** *Uncle* **Christmas!**'

Rudolph nuzzled against his shoulder and stamped his front feet up and down with a *CLUMP CLUMP*.

'Yes, don't worry, I haven't forgotten the flying dust,' Harry laughed. The magic dust was kept in a cupboard high up on one wall, with an enchantment on the door which meant that it **only opened on Christmas Eve**. Harry grinned to see the door open now, and the jar of special dust glowing brightly from where it stood on the shelf. He remembered the thrill of seeing his mum smear the dust onto the reindeer hooves back when he was a little boy – and now it was *his* turn to work the magic!

Carefully he unscrewed the lid of the jar and a silvery sparkling light streamed out from inside. Then he crouched down beside Rudolph, dipped his finger in the warm, tingling dust and gently rubbed it around each of his hooves: one, two, three, four. Rudolph's hooves glittered and gleamed. 'Up!' cried Harry to check the magic had worked and Rudolph flew off the ground and trotted around in mid-air. 'Brilliant!' Harry said, beaming.

He went from reindeer to reindeer, applying the magic dust to each one. Donner, Blitzen,

Dasher, Dancer . . . hoof by hoof, his flying team were coming together. Before long, there was only one reindeer left – Prancer – and then they would be ready to go.

'Your turn, pal,' said Harry, crouching beside Prancer, the jar of dust balanced on his knee. But just then –

'**We did it!**' came a yell, and into the stable burst Juniper and Wolfie, both looking wildly excited. Wolfie leaped up to lick Harry's face, paws on Harry's chest – but in his eagerness, managed to knock Harry right over, into the straw.

'Whoa!' yelled Harry in alarm as the jar of magic dust toppled off his knee. He lunged to catch it but – *too late!* – it bounced down to the ground and the dust spilt all over the straw. '**Oh *no***,' he gulped, trying to scoop it up. But the dust slipped through his fingers and fizzled out to nothing, leaving the jar completely empty.

Harry could hardly breathe. He turned hot and cold all over. The sleigh needed **eight reindeer** to pull it safely – and yet only *seven* of them could fly. What was he going to do?

CHAPTER FOUR

Horrified, Juniper put her face in her hands.

Wolfie's ears went down and he made an apologetic whimpering sound.

'I'm so sorry,' gulped Juniper. 'The last sack of presents has just been filled, and they're all ready to be put on the sleigh. Everyone's really proud and excited; I couldn't wait to tell you. But now . . .' She hung her head, not able to finish the sentence.

Harry actually felt a bit like crying. After all that hard work . . . and now it seemed as if they had fallen at the last hurdle. It took **a whole year** for the jar to fill up with magic dust again, so he couldn't exactly pop out to the shop and get any more. How were they going to deliver the presents with only seven reindeer?

Just then they heard a voice. '**Ho ho ho!**

Where's my sleigh? I'm ready to go!'

Harry swung round to see Nick, up and out of bed – and fully dressed in his Father Christmas outfit. 'W-w-what . . .' Harry stammered, '. . . are you doing?'

'Well, it's Christmas Eve, I need to get going,' said Nick, blowing his nose. 'This *is* my job, after all. I promised Mum and Dad I could do it. *I can't let them down!*'

'But I thought . . .' Harry said, dismay sinking through him. 'I thought . . . *I* was going to do it? As *Uncle* Christmas?'

'That was before, when I was . . . **AT*CHOO*!** . . . ill,' said Nick. Then he coughed and coughed, his face turning red. 'I'm fine now,' he wheezed.

'Nick, you're not fine, you're sneezing and coughing,' said Harry. 'Didn't Annie say you should stay in bed?'

But Nick paid no attention. He swung himself into the sleigh, grabbed the reins and opened his mouth as if he was about to call to the reindeer to set off straight away.

'**Wait!**' called Harry urgently. 'Prancer

isn't ready yet. We . . .' And then he turned bright red, because he knew Nick was going to be cross when he told him about spilling the magic dust. He might even think Harry had ruined Christmas, which would make him feel worse than ever. 'There's been a slight problem,' he confessed.

'What do you mean – **AT*CHOO*!** **AT*CHOO*!** – a problem?' Nick asked.

Wolfie slumped down into the straw and put a paw over one eye.

'Er . . .' said Harry, shuffling his feet about. 'Well . . .'

'**Look at Wolfie's paws**,' Juniper gasped suddenly, and they all stared. Even Wolfie himself held out a paw to inspect it and his furry eyebrows jumped to see the fur lit up with tiny golden sparkles.

Harry held his breath, remembering how the magic dust had spilt everywhere. Wolfie must have trodden in it! 'Do you think this means . . . ?' he asked, hardly daring to hope. Would the *flying* **magic** work the same way on a dog as it did on a reindeer?

Nick frowned. 'Is that glitter? I don't understand,' he said. 'What's going on?'

Juniper held up crossed fingers. 'Only one way to find out,' she said to Harry.

Harry swallowed, his heart pounding. He licked his lips. **'Wolfie? Up!'** he commanded.

They all stared as Wolfie wagged his tail and then leaped up into the air, where he galloped around above their heads, barking excitedly.

Harry burst out laughing. **'Brilliant!'** he cried in relief. 'Wolfie – you nearly ruined everything, but now you might just have saved the day. Or night, rather. Do you fancy being an honorary reindeer this Christmas Eve, and helping pull the sleigh?'

Wolfie's tail wagged so hard with excitement that he shot forward at top speed through the air, vanishing out of an open window with a startled *WOOF!* Then he zoomed back through the stable door, landing rather ungracefully on the ground, before running up to Harry and licking his face with extreme doggy eagerness.

'Okay!' Harry said, ruffling his fur. 'Well, that's that problem solved.'

'What about Prancer?' Nick asked, glancing over at the reindeer. But Prancer, who adored Harry, and realized the younger brother might be in trouble, gave a very dramatic shiver and faked a convincing cough. 'Ah,' said Nick as he gave a matching sneeze. 'You too, eh, buddy? Bad timing. All right, Wolfie, let's harness you up.'

They all went into the sleigh shed where the elves had loaded the sacks of presents onto the sleigh. Harry buckled his excited dog into the harness along with the reindeer, who were stamping their feet, impatient to get going. Then Nick sat down in the driving seat of the sleigh and took the reins.

'Are you *sure* you're well enough?' Harry

asked, unable to bear the fact that his Uncle Christmas experience was slipping away from him. 'I would really love to do it, Nick. **I know I can!**'

Nick gave a hacking cough. 'I just want to make sure everything goes well,' he fretted. 'I'm the one who's supposed to be Father Christmas – I've been preparing for it all year. Think of the children, Harry! I should go.'

'Yes, think of the children, *my feelings exactly*,' came a crisp, stern voice just then, and they all jumped as Annie walked into the shed looking *extremely* cross. 'Nicholas Christmas, what on *earth* do you think you're doing out of bed? Tell me you're not about to go around the world, spreading your nasty germs to all those poor boys and girls? You wouldn't be so silly, would you? **So *selfish*?**'

Nick's face crumpled a little. 'Well . . .'

'Thank goodness I popped by in time to stop you,' Annie went on, marching over and yanking the red hat from Nick's head. 'Because as your doctor, I absolutely forbid it. So give Harry the rest of the outfit – go on, hurry up! – and get yourself straight back to bed. **No arguments!**'

Nick sighed unhappily but he did as he was told. He peeled off the Father Christmas clothes looking miserable, and handed them to Harry. 'Good luck,' he said glumly before sneezing three times and trudging back out of the stable in the pyjamas he'd been wearing underneath. Harry felt sorry for him. He knew how much his brother had been looking forward to the **Big Night**. He had been *thrilled* last year when their dad said he was going to retire.

'Quickly! Before you freeze to death!' Annie called after Nick. 'I'll be in to check up on you in a minute.' Then she winked at Harry. 'All yours, **Uncle Christmas**.'

With a grateful smile, Harry pulled on the jacket and trousers, buckled his belt and put the red hat on his head. It all fitted perfectly. But Nick's words kept ringing through his head – *I'm the one who's supposed to be Father Christmas!* – and he hesitated, suddenly doubtful. This was the biggest, most responsible and grown-up thing he'd ever had to do in his life! 'I hope I can manage this,' he mumbled in a low voice.

'You can!' cried Juniper encouragingly. **'You'll do a great job**.'

Wolfie barked as if agreeing, and Prancer laid his head reassuringly on Harry's shoulder.

'*Of course* you can do it,' Annie said. 'Have a great time – and listen, don't you worry about your brother. I'll have a word with him.' She winked again at Harry. 'I'm the youngest in my family too. Sometimes you just have to prove the older ones wrong.'

Harry settled himself into the driving seat of the sleigh while the seven reindeer and one dog stood patiently. Through the open doors of the shed he could see the vast dark sky, spangled with silver stars, while a crowd of elves had gathered, waiting to wave him off. He cleared his throat, feeling tingly with excitement. This was his big moment. *You'll have the best night of your life on Christmas Eve, you really will!* he remembered his mum saying on the phone.

'**Up!**' he commanded boldly. Then the reindeer – and *Wolfie!* –

all kicked out

their legs and, with a flurry of magic silver sparkles, away they flew into the frosty black night.

*

So many rooftops, so many chimneys, so many fireplaces and creaky floorboards and stockings! The hours seemed to pass in a blur as the reindeer flew from country to country, house to house. Harry delivered presents to **hundreds and hundreds** of children who were all happily dreaming of magic.

They crossed the baking red outback of Australia and soared over the snowy mountains of Switzerland. They visited skyscrapers and bungalows, caravans and castles, igloos, tents and palaces. They flew to islands, the highlands;

over oceans and forests and through all the sleeping cities.

It was *so exciting* – the world was such a wonderful place! Harry felt dazzled by all the lovely messages and thank-you cards that children had left out. The mince pies on plates, the carrot tops for the reindeer! Harry felt sure he was the luckiest person in the whole world to be out on this most special of nights, carrying out *the* most special of jobs. He loved every minute of it!

Mind you, there were a few tricky moments along the way. A trio of triplets had all swapped beds and stockings to try and **confuse** Father Christmas. One little boy was so determined to stay awake that he had fallen asleep sitting up by his window, and Harry had to hold his breath while he carefully lifted him back into bed. And one very cheeky girl had booby-trapped the door, hoping the noise would wake her up so she could meet Father Christmas. Luckily for Harry, he knew all the *naughtiest* tricks and managed to tiptoe in and leave everyone's presents in the right places each time. **Phew!**

As for Wolfie, he was the best reindeer-dog ever. He loved galloping through the sky, his feathery tail wagging non-stop and even used his brilliant tracking skills to guide them across a misty moorland when Harry thought they might be lost. There was only one tiny near-disaster when they landed on a rooftop and Wolfie spotted a **squirrel** in a tree below.

For a moment, he forgot he was attached to the sleigh, and tried to leap towards the squirrel, almost pulling the sleigh and reindeer with him! Harry managed to haul on the rein to stop him just in time.

*

Then, before they knew it, the night was over. The sun was rising as Harry guided the reindeer and Wolfie safely back home, the sky striped with rose, orange and violet; the colours of dawn. Owls hooted softly from the forest to welcome them in, and the elves came rushing out of their homes to cheer the sleigh down once more. Harry waved at them, unable to stop beaming. **'We did it! We did it!'** he cried happily as he landed the sleigh in the crisp morning snow. 'Happy Christmas, everyone. You're all superstars. *You made Christmas happen!*' Then he jumped out, and was surrounded by the delighted elves, all wanting to hug him and pat Wolfie and hear how the night had gone.

Harry hugged them back, feeling thoroughly proud of himself – and even prouder of the elves, reindeer and Wolfie. '**What a team**,' he kept saying joyfully. 'What an absolutely brilliant team!'

But then he glanced over at the Christmas house, where the curtains were still drawn and he felt a prickle of dread. The last time he'd seen Nick, his brother had been trudging off back to bed, thoroughly disappointed to have

71

missed his big moment. How Harry hoped Nick would be pleased for him, after everything. All he'd ever really wanted was for Nick to say well done.

The reindeer were **yawning** and stamping their feet tiredly, so Harry took them to the stable to rub them down and put them to bed. Wolfie looked worn out after all that flying too, and flopped down in his dog basket with a happy little whiffle of his whiskers. Tiptoeing through the quiet house, Harry **collapsed** into his own bed, where within seconds he had fallen fast asleep with a great big smile on his face.

CHAPTER FIVE

After a lovely long snooze, Harry awoke to see that he'd had his very own Christmas visitor. Because there on the table beside his bed was a tray of breakfast and a pot of tea, complete with a **North Pole FC** tea cosy that Biff had knitted for him years before. Harry blinked a few times. Had last night really happened? he wondered dreamily.

'Ah, you're awake,' said Nick, popping his head around the door. '**Merry Christmas, Harry**. Breakfast should still be hot.'

Harry blinked. 'Thank you,' he mumbled, sitting up in bed and realizing that, in his tiredness last night, he'd forgotten to take off the red Father Christmas hat. So last night *had* happened then. 'Feeling better, are you?' he asked his brother, pulling the hat off his head.

'Much better, thanks,' said Nick. His smile was rather awkward as he sidled into the room. **'Um . . . sorry about last night.** I just so wanted to be Father Christmas. I wasn't thinking straight.'

Harry plonked the breakfast tray on his lap and began tucking in. He'd never felt so *hungry!* 'Don't worry about it,' he said through a mouthful of eggy toast. 'Here,' he added, passing the red hat over to Nick.

'You'd better have this back.'

Nick perched on the end of the bed looking sheepish. 'I felt **jealous** too,' he confessed. 'That you got to be Father Christmas first. But Annie was right: I was being selfish.'

'It's fine,' Harry told him. 'You'll get to do it next year – and every year after that! But from now on, I'm here to help, and the elves want to help again too.' He couldn't hold back a small proud grin as he remembered how crazy things had been over the last few days. 'We made some pretty good presents, actually. I hope the children like them when they wake up this morning.'

'Like them? **They love them!**' Nick replied. 'I've been checking the **Tinselnet** –

there are **Record Levels of Joy** around the world. Millions and millions of extremely happy children. It was a huge success, Harry. *Huge!*'

Harry's smile grew even wider. 'Oh brilliant!' he cried. 'I'm so pleased! But you need to take some credit too,' he pointed out. 'Don't forget all those presents that you slaved away to make as well. **You were working non-stop** since January. I only did a few days of work – and that was tough enough.'

Nick wrinkled his nose. 'Yeah,' he agreed, 'but I've been looking at the data breakdown and the children are happiest in houses where they got to open *your* presents. Presents that you and the elves made, rather.' He gave a sad little laugh. 'Turns out that not everyone really loves chess sets and jigsaw puzzles as much as me, after all.'

'But some children do!' Harry reminded him. '*Lots* of children do! They like different things, that's all. And some of the boys and girls wrote letters *asking* for chess sets and jigsaw puzzles. They'll be thrilled to unwrap the ones you made, I bet.'

Nick nodded but his face was still a bit sad.

'Listen, I've been thinking,' he said after a moment. 'You were a great **Uncle Christmas** this year –

but maybe . . .' He broke off, as if the words were hard to say. 'Maybe you should be **Father Christmas** next year,' he went on quietly and passed the red hat back to Harry. 'And every year. You'll do a better job than me.'

Harry almost dropped his knife and fork in surprise. '**Are you serious?**' he asked, staring at the Father Christmas hat and then back up at his brother.

'You get on better with the elves,' Nick said. 'You're kind and generous, even to the children who have been a bit naughty. You make really fun toys. The reindeer would do anything for you . . .' He shrugged. 'Besides, I found the whole thing kind of *stressful* this year. I think that was what made me ill. I was scared

I wouldn't do as good a job as Dad did.'

Harry's mind was whirring. He thought about how it had felt to skim across the moonlit sky with Christmas magic shimmering around the world, how it had been the **most *wonderful night of his life***. But then he remembered how his brother had been so excited about becoming Father Christmas himself, back when their dad had announced their retirement. Was it really fair to take that away from him?

'**Wow**,' he croaked. 'Nick . . . you are the nicest brother in the world. But you don't have to stop being Father Christmas. Because I know how much you wanted it too.'

'Well—' Nick began, but Harry was still talking.

'I agree that working too hard probably made you ill – but it was also because **I wasn't helping you enough**.' He felt his face grow hot, thinking about the many days and weeks when he'd been mucking about with the elves, while his brother slaved away in the workshop all on his own. 'I didn't even keep the house clean, let alone help you with the children's presents. I'm sorry about that.' He passed the hat back to Nick. 'It's your job. But I'll *help* you next time, and so will the elves. I reckon we'll make a great team.'

Just then they heard a woof from downstairs. A rather disappointed-sounding woof. 'Everything all right, Wolfie?' called Harry, swallowing the last bit of eggy toast. He and Nick hurried downstairs to see that Wolfie was jumping up in the air . . . only to land back on the ground again.

WOOF! he went, looking puzzled.

'He's trying to **fly** again,' Harry realized, ruffling his fur with a chuckle. 'Oh, Wolfie, I'm afraid the Christmas magic is over now for another year.' He grinned at Nick. 'Still, if a reindeer ever falls ill in future, we've got a willing replacement right here.'

Nick patted Wolfie. 'Good to know,' he laughed, and then peered out of the window. 'It's very *quiet* out there,' he commented. 'I don't know where the elves are this morning, do you?'

Harry thought for a moment, then smiled,

remembering his discovery the week before. 'I bet I know *exactly* where they are,' he said, and went to quickly get dressed. 'Wolfie, are you coming?' he called as he came back downstairs again. 'Follow me,' he told Nick.

And so off the three of them went, hurrying through the snow all the way into the forest where – yes! Harry had guessed right – the elves were whizzing down the ice slide together, shrieking and giggling, having the best fun ever.

'Wheeeeee!'

'Woohoo!'

'Wahey!'

*'**Whoop-dee-doo!**'* they squealed, zooming around the icy bends at top speed before flying head first into

a snowdrift at the bottom. **FLUMP!**

Wolfie wasted no time in bounding over to the slide himself, his ears flapping up as he hurtled down the slope. Harry and Nick rushed over too. Nick whizzed down first and Harry threw himself after his brother, both of them laughing with glee as they flew down the slope together.

ZOOM!
   ZOOM!
      WHIZZ!

'Merry Christmas!' yelled Nick joyfully

at the top of his voice. Harry couldn't remember seeing his brother look so carefree before. It suited him!

'**This is the best Christmas EVER!**' cried Harry, laughing as the slide came to an end and he shot straight into a heap of snow at the bottom. He rolled onto his back and made snow angels, gazing up at the sky and remembering what it had been like to fly through the starry darkness the night before. He thought about all those children waking up to find stockings full of presents at the end of their beds and felt a sizzle of happiness that he'd helped make that happen.

All in all, it was a **very lovely Christmas Day** at the North Pole that year and they all had a wonderful time. But Harry knew he would never forget the extra-special night when he had to become Uncle Christmas and save the day. And nor would Wolfie!

THE END

GRANNY
CHRISTMAS

CHAPTER ONE

It was the following December, and all was well up in the frozen north. Snow twinkled on the treetops, the forest animals were snug and cosy in their dens, and the air glittered with Christmas magic. The houses were strung with sparkly fairy lights and colourful streamers, while the kitchens smelled of warm mince pies and cinnamon. And over at the **Christmas workshop**, the sound of happy elvish singing could be heard as the toy-making team worked their warm woolly socks off.

Everyone was busy in there. Cherry and Pip were baking vanilla buns for afternoon tea, while Candy and Ginger shaped colourful sweets. Ribbons and Pine were hard at work on the sewing machines, stitching and stuffing teddies, dolls and cuddly toys. Noel and Mistletoe were making basketballs and scooters, while Jingle boinged around, testing pogo sticks. Juniper and Perky were leading a team of elves making wooden toys, sawing, carving and painting. As for Nick and Harry Christmas, they were wrapping presents and ticking each one off a great big list.

But wait a minute. What was this, zooming through the air towards the Christmas house?

Wheeeeeeeee!

BANG! *SMASH!* THUD!

'Whoa!' cried Harry in alarm. 'What was that?'

The elves stopped singing then rushed over to the window. 'It's a giant red . . . bird?!' Rudy said doubtfully, staring wide-eyed.

Then Harry and Nick heard a loud, rather cross-sounding squawk – *AARRRRK!* – followed by a voice saying, 'Whoopsie-daisy!'

They stared at one another in surprise. **'GRANNY?'** they both said, leaping up and dashing outside. Wolfie the dog immediately charged after them, his feathery tail wagging excitedly. The last time they'd seen **Granny Christmas**, she'd had an ancient bit of mackerel in her handbag which she'd given to him. This was the joyful sort of moment that a dog *never* forgot.

Out in the yard, they found a scene of complete chaos. A small red plane had plunged nose first into a snowdrift, its back propeller still spinning as thick black smoke poured from the engine. A penguin wearing a scarf was waddling around, looking extremely grumpy.

'ARK,' it squawked in a peevish sort of way. And a woman with silvery hair spilling out from her big fur cap was taking off a pair of flying goggles and beaming.

'**Boys!**' she cried, waving as she tramped through the snow towards them. 'Thought I'd drop in for a cup of tea. Sorry about the racket. The ground took me rather by surprise.'

'Hello, Granny!' said Nick, rushing over to give her a hug.

'Good to see you!' Harry said happily. She smelled of pear drops and had a surprisingly crushing cuddle. 'Are you okay? That sounded like a **bumpy** landing.'

Wolfie, meanwhile, had stopped wagging his tail and was staring suspiciously at the penguin.

Having lived his whole life near the North Pole, he'd never seen a creature from the *South* Pole before and he bared his teeth at the black and white bird with a low **growl**. The penguin clicked its beak and made a **hissing** sound in reply.

'Percy, don't be shy,' Granny cooed, tickling him under his chin. Then – **the horror!** – she plucked a rancid fish head from her bag and gave it to the penguin *and not to Wolfie*. 'I'm fine, thank you, dearie,' she said, turning back to Harry and not noticing as the dog let out a sad little whine. 'Just a wee bump on the bonce. I'll be right as rain after a nice hot cup of tea. Eh, boys?'

Some of the elves had come out to see the visitors, and Granny clapped her hands at the sight of them. 'Hello there, darlings! Remember me? Granny Christmas from the South Pole. Anyone want a sweetie?'

'Me!' 'Yummy!' 'Yes please!' cried the elves at once, who had *very* sweet tooths. They rushed over immediately as Granny rummaged in her pockets, then pulled out a large bag of striped humbugs.

'Now, no pushing,' she warned as some jostling and elbowing started up. '**There's plenty for everyone**!'

Nick looked at Harry with a grin. 'I'll put the kettle on,' he said.

*

A short while later, Nick, Harry and Granny were settled comfortably around the Christmas kitchen table, with cups of tea and warm cinnamon buns. Snow fell silently in big soft flakes and Wolfie, feeling tired, padded across towards his fireside bed. Then he stopped.

And growled. Because there, in *his* bed, was that annoying grumpy penguin. Fast asleep!

Granny giggled when she realized what had happened. 'Oh, Percy, **you cheeky boy!** He's made himself right at home,' she said, then bent down to ruffle Wolfie's fur. 'You don't mind, do you, old chap? He's worn out, you see. We've had an *extremely* long journey.'

Wolfie *did* mind. He minded very much. But he was a good dog, so he lay down on the cold stone floor instead with only the smallest of whiskery huffs.

'What are you even doing here, Granny?' Harry asked, topping up her teacup. 'I mean – it's **lovely** to see you, but we weren't expecting you.'

'Oh! Were you not? That's strange,' said Granny. 'I did pop a letter in the post to you as we left the Sahara the other day. Unless . . .' She frowned and delved into her handbag. Then she pulled out an unopened, unposted envelope along with a small shower of sand that pattered onto the floor. '**Whoops**. I must have forgotten to post it,' she chuckled. 'Here it is, anyway. It says, Beloved Grandsons, I'll be with you on Tuesday at four o'clock for a cup of tea and a chat.' She checked her watch. 'Ten past four. Look at that, I was right on time!'

Nick smiled. He and Harry were very fond of their granny. She had always been full of surprises! 'Are you staying for Christmas?' he asked. 'You're welcome to join us, if you'd like. Mum and Dad are on another winter cruise, so there's plenty of space.'

'I don't want to be any bother!' Granny cried in reply. 'I'm just having a wee adventure, you know, flying around the world. Me and my penguin, seeing the sights. Once I've checked over the plane, I'll be out of your hair, boys. You'll hardly know I've even been here.'

'There's no hurry,' Harry said. 'You can stay for as long as you like. We'd love to have you and Percy here. In fact, I . . .' He stopped talking just then as a revolting smell drifted past his nostrils. '*Ugh*,' he coughed, fanning a hand in front of his face. 'What is *that*?'

'**Oops!** That'll be Percy,' said Granny, peering down at the snoozing penguin. 'Sorry about the pong. You get used to it after a while.'

While Harry opened a window to let in some fresh air, Nick asked Granny about her latest work. She was an **inventor**, and loved coming up with wild new creations. Not all of them had been completely successful though. For instance, when Nick and Harry had been very tiny, she had built a **Cot-Rocker** that was supposed to rock them gently to sleep at night. And did it work? Well, it rocked them . . . but not gently. In fact, it was more like a baby roller coaster . . . and instead of lulling them to sleep, it made sure they were wide awake. **WHEEEEE!** *WAHHHH!*

Then, when Nick and Harry were a bit older but still not very tall, Granny had kindly created some **Springy-Legz** for them, which meant they could reach things that were very high up. And did they work? Yes! Too well! Wearing the Springy-Legz, they were able to bounce right up to the biscuit tin in the top cupboard of the kitchen . . . **BOING! BOING!** . . . and help themselves to every last crumb. Their mum and dad had not been too pleased about *that*.

There had also been the time when Granny had given Nick and Harry's parents a special Christmas present . . . a painting robot.

'I know you don't have much time for decorating, with all your Christmas work,' she'd said, 'so meet the **BrushBot** who's going to help you out.' And did the BrushBot work? Oh yes. It painted the walls . . . and the windows . . . and the doors . . . and the furniture . . . in fact, the BrushBot actually began painting *Harry* when he stood too close to it, until his mum decided that the BrushBot had done quite enough painting for that day and pressed its 'Off' button. Shortly after that,

Nick and Harry's parents had politely said, **No More Inventions, Thank You** to Granny.

'Well!' Granny said now, pleased to be asked. 'I've been working on my new plane which is a splendid wee thing. There's a built in tea-maker, for when Percy and I get thirsty, there's an automatic slipper-warmer, for chillier flights, and there's a **special water pistol** at the front that Percy uses to squirt naughty seagulls. The only problem is that the landing controls can be a bit hit and miss, as you might have noticed.' She waggled her eyebrows. 'Today was definitely a case of "hit", unfortunately.'

'Never mind,' Nick said. 'As long as you and Percy are okay, that's the main thing.'

'Och, we're fine!' said Granny. 'Now, if

someone could lend me a screwdriver, I'll just go and tighten up a few nuts and bolts, and smooth out the plane's nose. Then we'll be on our way.'

But just as she was getting to her feet, there was an almighty *BOOM!* from outside.

The windows rattled. The fairy lights blinked in surprise. Wolfie's ears pricked up. Even Percy opened a beady yellow eye and gave a fishy-smelling hiss.

'What on earth . . . ?' Granny yelped, hurrying to the window . . . just in time to see her beloved plane go up in flames. '**No!**' she cried in dismay.

'Oh dear,' said Harry as a blackened water pistol fell from the cockpit and landed, sizzling in the snow.

'There goes Percy's pistol!' groaned Granny.

Wheee! A burning kettle flew out of the back seat and exploded with a loud POP.

'Not my tea-maker as well!' wailed Granny.

Then the pilot's door fell off with a CLUNK-*THUD*, and a pair of scorched fluffy slippers dropped from the footwell, **plop plop**, with smoke gushing from their toes.

'Well, I won't be wearing *those* again,' Granny sighed. 'Dearie me. Now I *am* in a pickle.'

'Looking on the bright side,' said Nick. 'You can stay with us for a bit longer after all.'

CHAPTER TWO

Granny was pretty sure that the plane's explosion had been caused by her forgetting to switch off her built-in slipper-warmer. **Bother!** Still, by a stroke of luck, her small red suitcase had been blown out of the back of the plane and landed in a heap of snow, completely unharmed. So had Percy's smaller blue suitcase. So Granny was able to unpack her clothes and toothbrush when she moved into the Christmas brothers' spare room, and Percy could unpack his surprisingly *large* collection of scarves and waistcoats. In honour of their visitors, Nick cooked a special dinner that evening, while Harry cut armfuls of holly and ivy, and decorated the place with them. Soon the house looked and smelt festive and jolly, and they were all having a **lovely** time.

All of them, that is, apart from Wolfie. Surely *everyone* knew that a dog's place during meals was under the table, ready to pounce on dropped crumbs or – if he was lucky – a whole

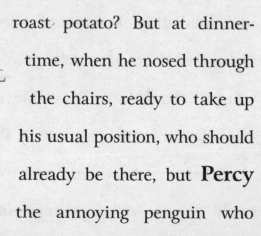

roast potato? But at dinnertime, when he nosed through the chairs, ready to take up his usual position, who should already be there, but **Percy** the annoying penguin who hissed at him and then – **of all the cheek!** – stuck out his long beak and *pecked* him.

Wolfie yelped in surprise and barked at Percy. Stealing Wolfie's bed had been bad enough, but pecking was another thing altogether!

Hearing the bark, Granny peered under the table. '**Wolfie!** Don't you be mean to my Percy!' she warned, wagging a finger. 'There's plenty of room under there for both of you.'

Even Harry didn't stick up for his dog. 'Come on, mate, you're much bigger than him, there's no need to bark,' he said, ruffling Wolfie's fur. 'Give Percy a bit of space, he's probably feeling shy, being in a strange place.'

Shy, indeed, thought Wolfie crossly, slinking away. There were plenty of words he could use about that penguin, but 'shy' was not one of them. **Humph**. Well, at least he had his bed back again, he supposed.

But then, as he reached his bed, his nose twitched, and not in a good way. **It *stank!*** There were even a few oily black and white feathers in there, as if Percy was turning it into his own nest. Wolfie stared in dismay, then turned away, tail between his legs. A dog had his dignity. And Wolfie was not going to sleep *there* any more.

Feeling very fed up, Wolfie went and lay in front of the warm oven instead, keeping a watchful eye on his new enemy. He hoped Percy wouldn't be staying long. The **sooner** that penguin headed back to the South Pole, the better!

*

The next morning, the plane had stopped burning and lay like a cold black skeleton in the snow. After breakfast, Nick headed over to the workshop, to start making that day's presents with the elves. Meanwhile, Granny and Harry went out to inspect the damaged plane, with Percy waddling after them. Wolfie slunk along behind, keeping a safe distance.

'**Let's see** . . .' said Granny, licking the end of a pencil and starting a list in her notepad. 'So she's going to need some new wings, that's for sure. And a new tail. New windows. New doors. New seats. A new control panel. A new engine. A new nose-cone. And new wheels. That's before we've even thought about our luxuries.'

'*ARRRK!*' squawked Percy, pecking at one of the blackened seats.

'Yes, that's right, and a new cushion for Percy,' Granny added. 'He does like to be comfortable on a long flight. Don't we all?'

Harry bit his lip. Granny's plane had been completely destroyed. What terrible luck. 'So you're going to have to start again, really,' he said gently, hoping she wasn't too disappointed. **Poor Granny!** He couldn't help feeling sorry for her. He could tell that she'd really loved her creation.

'Yes,' said Granny, tucking her pencil back behind her ear. 'I'll have to build a new one completely from scratch.' Then she clapped her hands together with a huge smile. '*Whoopee!*

What a treat. Building things is the best fun ever – and my next plane will be even better than before, just you wait!' She began another list in her notepad. 'First things first, I'll have to draw up some plans,' she said. 'I'm going to need paper. Different-coloured pens. A large workspace. Some funky music to listen to. And quite a lot of biscuits, I should think.'

Harry blinked. Granny was taking all of this very well. In fact, she looked positively delighted to have a new project on her hands! 'No problem,' he told her.

'I'll have to give my pal in the **Antarctic Plane Parts Warehouse** a call too,' she said, marching back towards the house in a determined sort of way. 'Let him know that I need supplies.' She stamped the snow off her boots as they reached the front door and twinkled her eyes at Harry. 'And don't worry, dearie, I know you and Nick are very busy, so I'll make sure I keep well out of your way. Quiet as a mouse and no trouble, that's me.'

'Granny, it's fine, we **love** having you here,' Harry told her with a laugh. 'We've got plenty of paper, pens and biscuits – and lots of helpful elves as well, if you need an extra hand. And me too, of course! I've never seen a plane being built – it sounds **really cool**.'

'Oh, it will be!' cried Granny. 'And I'd be delighted to have a new assistant. So what are we waiting for? We've got work to do.'

Granny wasted no time in drawing up plans for a brand-new aeroplane and ordering all the equipment she would need. It was an **extremely long list**.

Over the next few days, some exciting-looking parcels arrived. Some huge sheets of metal. A collection of wheels. Two seats. A whole box of levers and buttons. And several types of fabric, so that Percy could choose one for his cushion. Soon, the barn that Granny was using as her workshop filled up, and she was kept very busy.

As for Harry, her assistant, he was learning all sorts of things. And Granny was right – building a plane *was* fun!

Granny taught him how to cut the metal down to size using a machine that made a *lot* of noise.
SCREECH! ROAR! WHINE!

They tramped out to the pine forest together, where they cut down a tree –
TIMBERRRRRR! –
then Granny demonstrated how to nail pieces of wood into a cabin shape. **BANG!** *WALLOP!* **CRASH!**

Granny also showed Harry how to make a pair of seats for the cabin, and then set him to work cutting fabric for cushions. **SNIP! SNIP! SNIP!** Meanwhile, she made a

little pull-down blind for Percy's window for when the sun was too bright *B Z Z Z Z Z Z!* went the sewing machine. ***BZZZZZ!***

Best of all, Granny handed Harry a pair of welding goggles and taught him how to make a brand-new nose-cone for the plane with a really cool welding gun that ***ROARRRRR**Red* with flames. It was absolutely brilliant!

But not everyone was quite so happy, unfortunately. During this time, the elves had noticed a few things going missing from the Christmas workshop and as a result, the toy-making kept grinding to a halt.

'Where are my **woodworking tools?**' cried Juniper, seeing her bare work bench.

'Has anyone moved my **sewing machine?**' asked Pine, hunting around.

'What happened to all the **paints and brushes?**' exclaimed Noel, blinking at the sight of the empty cupboard.

'And who keeps eating the **shortbread?**' grumbled Cherry, opening the biscuit tin to find just a few crumbs left inside.

Nick had a pretty good idea who was disrupting things and went out to find Granny in her workshop. She was in there with Harry, and sure enough was surrounded by Juniper's tools, using

Pine's sewing machine, with Noel's paints and brushes nearby. *And* Granny was munching her way through a plate of elvish shortbread. Hmmm!

'Um . . . Granny,' Nick said politely, 'the elves need their equipment back. They can't work without it.'

'Whoops! Sorry!' Granny cried, leaping up at once. 'I'll help you take it all back. Perfect timing actually, because I've just finished Percy's cushion for the new plane. Come and see what we've been doing, we've been ever so busy in here.'

'Very nice,' Nick said as she and Harry showed him the wings they had built, then the tail, and finally the cockpit. The cockpit had flowery wallpaper, comfortable seats, and an excellent new slipper-warmer with an automatic switch-off function. There was even space for a snazzy tea-maker and a special holder for a biscuit tin.

'Now I just need my **new engine** to arrive,' Granny said, once they had finished the tour. 'According to my pal in the South Pole, there's a delivery delay, and it could take another week or so to get here. Rather annoyingly, we can't start putting the plane together without it.'

'I see,' said Nick, although his heart sank just a tiny bit. Much as he *loved* his granny, he really did need to keep things ticking along in the workshop. He hoped she wasn't going to cause any more problems around the place!

CHAPTER THREE

Whatever Nick might think, Granny Christmas did *not* want to cause problems. In fact, while she waited for her new engine to arrive, she wanted to help her grandsons and make them happy. What better way to do that, she thought, than by baking a **delicious** home-made cake?

And so she and Percy went off to the kitchen and, with matching aprons and chef hats, they were soon busily weighing out flour, butter and chocolate, and taking it in turns to stir the mixture. But when Granny's back was turned, naughty Percy decided to make the cake rather more to a penguin's taste, by sneaking two smelly old fish into the bowl.

Granny's nose twitched a bit as she gave the cake mix one final stir and poured it into a tin to bake, but she thought the fishy pong was probably just coming from Percy. That was where most fishy pongs came from, after all.

Into the oven went the cake, and when it was cooked, Granny cut it into slices, and took it round the workshop, offering everyone a piece. And was it **delicious?** No, it was *not*.

'*Ugh*,' choked the elves as they tasted the fishy chocolate cake.

'*Yuck*,' said Nick, his eyes watering at the first mouthful.

'*Whoa!*' cried Harry, plucking something from his teeth. 'There are *bones* in this cake. Fish bones!'

Nick spat the cake into his hand. '**And a fish . . . *eye*!**' he gulped.

121

'Dearie me,' said Granny in surprise. 'However did *that* get in there?' She caught sight of Percy shuffling quickly away, and giggled. 'Oh, Percy, you wee monkey. Playing tricks on us like that! Sorry, everyone. Still – no harm done, eh?'

But unfortunately for Granny, harm *had* been done. Because that night, everyone felt **very poorly indeed**. By the next morning, Nick and Harry had just about recovered but the elves still felt so unwell that Nick had to call for Doctor Annie.

When Annie arrived, she told the elves to stay in bed for the rest of the day and so Nick and Harry had to work **extra hard** in the workshop to try and keep on top of everything. Even Wolfie did a share of the work by towing finished toys and gifts along in a cart to be wrapped. Meanwhile, Granny was feeling terrible for causing such chaos.

'I *am* sorry,' she said, filling hot-water bottles for the poorly elves. 'Now we're in a proper pickle, aren't we? Dearie me!'

While Nick, Harry and Wolfie were busy in the workshop, Granny wandered around looking for ways to be helpful. 'If only there was something **really wonderful** we could do, Percy, to cheer everyone up again,' she murmured. 'Let me think . . .'

Perhaps they shouldn't try any more baking, she decided regretfully – and Percy was scared of the hoover, so a good old clean-up was out of the question too. Then, as she gazed out of the window, her eye fell on the sleigh shed and a brilliant new idea popped into her head. '**Ah, I know!**' she said, clapping her hands together. 'I'll get the sleigh all ready for Christmas Eve, run a few tests on the old thing to make sure it's working properly. Won't Nick and Harry be pleased? Come on, Percy! We've an important job to do.'

'A*ARRRKKK!*' said Percy, waddling behind as she hurried off there immediately.

Once at the shed, Granny got straight to work. Humming to herself, she peeled off the sleigh's protective covers, plucked out a few **spiders** who had set up cobwebby homes there, then stood back to give it a long beady look.

'Hmmm,' she said, noticing a small tear in the

front seat, a crack in the rear present-guard, and some rather scuffed paintwork. 'Those boys have not been looking after you very well, have they? Don't you look sad and neglected and . . . well, no offence, but sort of boring, actually. There's some work to do here, all right, Percy. **Time to jazz this sleigh well and truly** *up*!'

*

After some seriously hard work all day, Nick, Harry and Wolfie emerged from the workshop feeling tired and hungry. Between them, they had made and wrapped all sorts of lovely presents – and tested out quite a few **tennis balls**, in Wolfie's case – but they hadn't been able to do nearly as much as they would have done if the elves had been there to work alongside them. 'I hope they're all feeling better tomorrow,' said Nick, glancing over at their little houses. 'It's not the same without them.'

'It's **so quiet** too,' Harry said.

'It's *really* quiet,' Nick agreed as they tramped across the snow. 'I wonder what Granny has been doing all day?'

'**Look!** I can see something going on in the sleigh shed,' Harry said, pointing to where a light was shining out of the window. 'She must be in there.'

They hurried across to see her, hoping she hadn't been too bored while they'd been so busy. But as soon as they walked into the sleigh shed, it was clear that Granny hadn't been bored at all. '**Ah, there you are!**' she cried happily. 'I thought I'd clean this old girl up a bit. Doesn't she look better for some paint and polish?'

Staring at the sleigh, Nick opened his mouth then shut it again, as if he didn't know what to say. '**Wow**,' was all that he could croak. Because the sleigh looked *very* different from how it had done before.

Fluffy cushions now adorned the seats. Fairy lights twinkled from the present-guard bar at the back. There was a new built-in oven – 'Handy for warming up a mince pie!' twinkled Granny – and a stereo system that played Granny's favourite funky beats. She turned the volume down a little, beaming proudly.

'**What do you think?**' she asked, when

neither Nick nor Harry responded. 'Much cosier

now, wouldn't you say? And lots more fun!'

'**AARRRKKK!**' squawked Percy, buffing up

the front of the sleigh with a wing.

Nick shook his head. Harry bit his lip. Wolfie let out a little whine. Neither of the grandsons wanted to hurt their granny's feelings but they didn't quite know what to say.

'Boys?' prompted Granny.

'Er . . .' Harry began. 'Well . . . we can see you've worked really hard here, Granny, but . . .'

'But it can't stay like this, I'm afraid,' Nick finished. 'Everything has to go back **the way it was**, Granny. This is all wrong. The music will wake everyone up, you see – and the oven is probably a fire hazard, and . . .'

'I was just trying to make it a bit more *homely*,' Granny said, looking crestfallen. 'I thought you'd be pleased!'

'Thank you,' Harry said, hating to see her disappointment. 'But you see, the sleigh has looked the same way for hundreds of years – and that's how everyone likes it.'

Granny pursed her lips. 'But they'll like it this way too, I bet,' she said. 'And you will, as well! Who *doesn't* like a nice fat cushion on a long journey?'

'But this is not how the sleigh is meant to be!' Nick replied. He was starting to lose his patience. 'Check any Christmas card – it isn't supposed to have mince-pie ovens or cushions. Or fairy lights!'

'Ah,' Granny put in. 'Well, you see, those fairy lights are actually doing a very useful job there, holding the present-guard together.

I noticed a *crack* and so –'

But Nick wasn't listening. 'You'll have to put it all back the way it was, I'm afraid,' he said wearily. 'I'd better go and start making some dinner. Then feed the reindeer. Then check on the elves . . .'

'**But** –' Granny protested but Nick was already striding away, frowning as he murmured his list of chores to himself. Wolfie, meanwhile, who'd heard the word 'dinner' began nudging Harry in a hopeful sort of way.

Granny gave a sigh. 'Dearie me, and now I've upset you boys,' she said, gazing after Nick's retreating figure. 'When that was **the last thing** I wanted to do!'

'Don't worry,' said Harry kindly. 'He's just

tired, that's all, and there's a lot to do. It's been a long day.' Wolfie began pawing at his coat and Harry patted him. 'Just a minute, boy. I know you're hungry.' Then he turned to Granny again. 'Do you want me to give you a hand, putting everything back?'

'No, it's okay,' Granny said, as she began reluctantly removing all the sleigh's new accessories. 'Although maybe I should leave the fairy lights where they are – **you see they're actually there for a good reason** . . .'

But Wolfie was jumping up, trying to lick Harry's face and Harry was too distracted to listen properly. 'Whoa!' he laughed. 'All right, all right, you want your dinner, I get it!'

'So what should I do about the *fairy lights?*' Granny persisted.

'Oh,' said Harry, already halfway out of the door. 'You'd better take **everything** off like Nick said, I'm afraid. We'd better not argue with Father Christmas, right?'

'Right,' said Granny, uncertainly. Harry and Wolfie left, and she turned back to the sleigh with a little frown. 'I hope this is going to be all right, Percy,' she said, 'but I suppose the boys know best. **Oh dear!** I'm causing trouble everywhere I go today. If only there was a way I could make it up to everyone!'

Hearing laughter, she glanced out of the window to see Harry throwing a snowball and Wolfie jumping up to catch it in his mouth.

Granny smiled . . . and just then, another brilliant idea popped into her head.

'**Of course!**' she laughed. 'I know the perfect thing. Tomorrow I'll make everything better with my best invention yet!'

CHAPTER FOUR

Peace and order returned to the Christmas workshop the next day. The elves had recovered and were **hard at work** once more, making new gifts and singing along to Christmas songs. Annie had popped by to check up on everyone, and was lending a hand by inspecting the junior doctor kits. Nick was ticking presents off his list and starting to feel calmer. The sleigh now looked exactly as it should do again and – **best of all** – Granny was quietly working on some new invention or other, and not causing any problems.

Phew! Nick thought. They were still on track to make it a great Christmas. It was all going to be absolutely fine.

But just then he heard a clanking noise from outside. Then a strange sort of whirring. And then came the sound of Granny's excited voice calling, 'Cooee! Where are you all? Who wants a snowball fight? Catch me if you can!'

There was a soft *FLUMP* of snow at the workshop window. Harry peered outside and burst out laughing. 'Oh my goodness,' he chuckled. **'This is amazing!** Come and see what she's built now!'

The elves wasted no time in following him out into the snow, where a very unusual sight met their eyes. Granny was strapped into a robot

that had four long metal
legs and seven arms,
each with giant
scoops for
hands at the
end. The robot was
running around,
shaping handfuls
of snow into
snowballs and
throwing them.

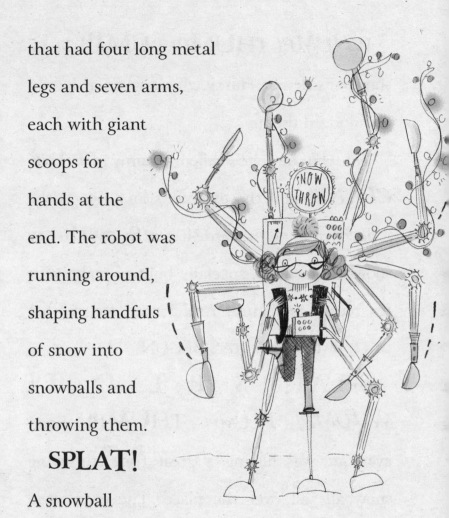

SPLAT!

A snowball
knocked Noel's hat off.

SPLOT! Another snowball bounced off
Berry's tummy.

WHUMP! **THUMP!** **BUMP!** Three snowballs flew at Harry who laughed as he ran and dodged them.

'Do you like it?' called Granny. ***CLANK CLANK*** went the machine's long legs as she walked it around the yard. 'It's my **SnowThrow** snowball machine, specially built to make your tea breaks more fun! And I now declare that this snowball fight HAS BEGUN!'

SPLAT! **S P L O T !** *WHUMP!* *FLUMP!* **THUMP!** Soon everyone was having a great time, throwing snowballs all over the place. The elves were pink-cheeked and breathless as they ducked and dodged, giggling and cheering whenever a snowball hit its target. Harry, Nick and Annie were enjoying themselves too, charging about, chucking snow at each other. As for Wolfie, he was leaping to catch snowballs in his mouth and barking excitedly, his tail wagging non-stop.

'What's really nifty,' called Granny above the din, 'is that I can make the SnowThrow throw teeny-tiny cutesy snowballs, nice and **soft** . . .' She flicked a switch to demonstrate and the SnowThrow began scooping baby snowballs and throwing them gently. 'Or,' Granny chortled, 'I can make it throw *mega* snowballs **hard** and fast.' She pressed a button and the SnowThrow whizzed into action, its metals arms a blur as they scooped and threw, snowball after snowball at top speed. But then . . .

sMASH! SHATTER! TINKLE! sMASH!

Some of the big, fast snowballs hurtled in the direction of the workshop . . . and smashed straight through the windows.

'**Stop!**' cried Nick in alarm. 'Granny, turn it off!'

'Oopsy!' said Granny, pressing a button. Nothing happened – apart from even more windows getting broken.

TINKLE! CRASH! sMASH!

'TURN IT OFF!' shouted Nick, and Granny frantically jabbed at all the levers, switches and buttons on her control panel. The SnowThrow began to dance around the yard, kicking snow into the air, its mighty robotic arms still throwing snowballs in all directions.

WHACK! Pine began
to cry as a speeding snowball
hit him right on the nose.

WHUMP!

Tinsel was knocked over
into a pile of snow and
shrieked with shock.

WALLOP! A massive snowball
sailed through a broken workshop window and
splattered all over the trays of lollipops left
cooling on a bench.

Finally, after a frantic bashing of the 'Off'
button, Granny managed to stop the Snow-
Throw. With a wheeze, its metal legs bent, it
lowered her to the ground and she unfastened

herself with trembling fingers. 'Dearie me,' she said in a small voice, staring at the motionless machine and then across at all the broken windows. 'I'm so sorry. I was only trying to have a bit of fun.'

Seeing she was upset, Harry put his arm round her. '**Don't worry**,' he said. 'Granny, you're shivering, let's go and make you a nice hot cup of tea. The SnowThrow machine is brilliant! But next time we'll remember not to use it near any windows.'

As the two of them went over to the house, Nick and Annie returned to the workshop and began sweeping up the shattered glass inside. Snowflakes tumbled softly through the broken windows and Biff, Juniper and Perky went to measure and put in new panes of glass. Meanwhile, Candy and Ginger had to throw away the snow-covered lollies and begin making another batch.

Nick could feel himself getting a teeny bit *stressed*. He really loved his granny but he was starting to hope her engine would be delivered soon, so that she could build her plane and let them finish their work. However nice it was to have her around, things had definitely been running **a lot smoother** before she'd arrived!

*

Outside, Wolfie was the only one left in the yard and he was just about to trot after Harry to warm up in front of the fire, when he heard a strange noise. A muffled *squawk*, rather small and frightened, coming from deep in the snow. 'AAARR*K! AA*RRR*K!*' Then there was an even smaller sound. 'EEEP!'

Now, everyone knows that dogs have **super-brilliant** ears and noses, and the noises certainly *sounded* as if they were coming from Wolfie's least favourite penguin . . . **but where was he?** Wolfie sniffed the air but all he could smell was snow. He gazed around but couldn't see Percy anywhere, just piles and piles of snowballs that the robot had thrown. Was Percy buried under one of them, maybe? Or was he being annoying and playing a silly trick?

Wolfie gave a gruff bark which was answered by a tiny, faint 'EEEP!' If Percy *was* playing a trick he sounded kind of anxious, Wolfie thought.

Frightened even. Wolfie put his super-brilliant nose to the ground and began to dig through the snow. 'EEEP!' went the sound again, barely a chirp now, and Wolfie dug faster, snow flying out from behind his big paws.

He barked again but no other sound came from Percy. Feeling worried, Wolfie dug even faster. He sniffed as hard as he could and could just detect a faint *fishy* penguin pong. He must be getting closer! Paws scrabbling, he dug deeper into the snow . . . **and at last found a flipper**.

Wolfie nudged at the flipper and barked again, but there was no response. He was starting to get a bad feeling about this. Even though he heartily disliked Percy and his bed-stealing, cake-wrecking, stinky ways, Wolfie did not want anything *too* terrible to happen to him.

He barked at the top of his voice to alert Harry and Granny. *WOOF! WOOF! WOOF!* Then he gave a blood-curdling howl for good measure. *AROOOOOOO!*

'Wolfie, whatever's the matter?' Harry called, hurrying out of the house as Wolfie tried to gently dig the rest of the snow off the penguin. 'Whoa – is that Percy?' Harry cried, running over. 'Oh, good dog. **Clever dog!**' he said as he helped Wolfie pull Percy free of the snow. 'Percy, can you hear me?' he asked, picking him up. 'Percy, mate, are you okay?' But the penguin just coughed and huddled closer to Harry, as if he was feeling very poorly indeed.

Hearing the commotion, Doctor Annie ran outside and took charge. She bundled Percy up in her coat and rushed him into the house, followed by Harry and Wolfie. '**Quick!** We need to warm him up. Fetch blankets! Hot-water bottles! **This is an *emergency*!**'

'Oh heavens!' cried Granny in alarm as they charged in. 'My little Percy-pops. Will he be all right?'

CHAPTER FIVE

Poor Percy was *not* all right – at least not at first.

He had caught a terrible case of the **penguin**

shivers, and had to stay in bed, wrapped up in

blankets and being fed mashed sardines every

two hours for quite a few days. Granny tended to

him lovingly, singing him his favourite penguin

songs and knitting him several new scarves and

jumpers – and the elves popped in with Get

Well Soon cards and some **flipper-warmers**

that they'd made. Even Wolfie felt a tiny bit

concerned about how ill his old enemy seemed.

Although Percy got on his nerves with all that pecking and squawking, life did feel strangely quiet without any penguin mischief going on.

Still, while Granny was busy caring for Percy, it did mean that Nick, Harry and the elves were able to catch up on all their **present-making** without any more interruptions. In fact, by Christmas Eve morning, the preparations for the **Big Night** looked pretty much perfect.

The presents had all been wrapped and packed.

Nick had washed and ironed his Father Christmas suit, and practised his best *HO HO HO!*s.

The jar of shimmering magic dust in the reindeer stable was full to the brim, all ready to be used on the reindeers' hooves that evening. (Wolfie was keeping a safe distance from it this year.)

And . . . **hooray!** Percy was out of bed at last, bright-eyed and looking *much* better. And the first thing he did was to shuffle over to Wolfie and fling his flippers around the dog's neck, as if to say thank you for rescuing him. Mind you, he couldn't resist giving Wolfie a *small friendly peck* a few minutes later, as well as doing a fishy-smelling penguin burp right in his ear, but Wolfie didn't mind too much. It was nearly Christmas after all.

'I think we're ready to go!' Nick called as the sun set that evening, and darkness filled the sky like a spreading ink blot. Looking splendid in his Father Christmas outfit, he strode out to the sleigh shed and began harnessing up the reindeer, helped by Harry. The elves carefully loaded the sacks of presents onto the sleigh and then Nick rubbed a pinch of **golden magic dust** onto each reindeer's hooves so that they were able to fly.

'Oh,' said Granny, appearing in the sleigh shed just then. 'You did remember to *mend* the rear present-guard, didn't you? It was a bit cracked the other day, so –'

But Nick was taking the reins and hadn't heard. '**UP!**' he commanded. The reindeer kicked out their legs and, with a flurry of magic silver sparkles, they galloped up into the frosty air and away.

'Good luck! See you tomorrow!' Harry called

as he and the elves waved them off, whooping

and whistling. **But wait!** What

was that? There was

a sudden loud

CRACK!

from above

their heads

and, by

the light

of the moon,

they saw something *break* on the back of the

sleigh . . . In the next moment, a huge sack of

presents had gone tumbling back down to Earth.

'Oh dear,' said Granny, biting her lip. 'I did

tell him. I did *say* that present-guard needing

fixing – and now it's snapped clean through!'

'Quick! Where did the sack land?' asked Harry anxiously as he raced across the snow. **'We've got to find those presents!'**

Nick, meanwhile, had circled the sleigh around and brought it back down to land. Jumping out, he ran through the darkness towards Harry. 'Where did they go?' he called.

'STOP!' shouted Harry, and Nick skidded to a halt, realizing just in time that Harry was standing at the edge of a sheer drop.

'It's no good,' Harry said glumly, pointing a torch down to where the sack had landed, right at the bottom. The sides of this valley were so steep that even the ***bravest*** of elves wouldn't sledge down there. 'If somehow we *do* manage to scramble down to get the presents, the snow is really deep. We might not be able to climb out again.'

Nick's head whirled with panic. He felt *terrible*. **'If only I'd listened to Granny,'** he said. 'She tried to warn me that the back of the sleigh was broken but I was in too much of a hurry to take any notice.' He gulped. 'If I can't deliver presents to all the children who deserve one then . . .' He shook his head unhappily. 'Then I'll have let everyone down. Christmas will be ruined!'

But just then, before Harry could reply, they both heard a strange sound. *CLANK CLANK*. *WHIRR*. Nick and Harry turned their heads, shining torches back towards the

Christmas house to see that there, striding through the snow on long metal legs was . . .

'Granny?'

'The SnowThrow!'

CLANK CLANK. WHIRR. Catching up with her grandsons, Granny grinned down at them, from where she was strapped into the robot. 'Ruin Christmas? Not on my watch,' she said. 'The SnowThrow also doubles up as a **PresentThrow** by the way. I hope you boys are good at catching!'

Nick and Harry watched open-mouthed as Granny strode all the way over to the edge of the valley. 'Please be careful!' Nick cried as she lowered one of the robot's long metal legs down, then another.

'Careful?' scoffed Granny. 'I'm always careful. Oopsie!' she shrieked in the very next minute as the SnowThrow's legs skidded on the snow and she was sent *plunging* all the way down to the bottom of the slope.

Harry gulped.

Nick gasped.

'Granny, are you all right?' they shouted in alarm.

'**Woohoo!**' Granny cried, getting back up on her feet. '**That was FUN.**' She waved all seven of the giant scoop hands at her grandsons. 'Don't look so worried. We grannies are tougher than you think. Now then, are you boys ready? Because here come the presents!'

She flicked a switch and . . .

SCOOP! SCOOP! SCOOP!
BOING! BOING! BOING!

The robot got to work, lifting and hurling the

brightly coloured gifts all the way up to Nick and Harry who caught them neatly, one by one. Up flew the sack too, and they quickly

repacked it full, good as new.

'Granny, you are the greatest,' called Harry

as the last present went sailing up to them. He caught it one-handed, popped it into the sack and cheered. **'You are an absolute Christmas superstar**. Do you want us to help you climb out of there? We could get a rope, or . . . ?'

'Nonsense! Of course I can manage,' said Granny, nimbly springing back up to join them again, thanks to the robot's long strong legs. 'I haven't had this much excitement since Percy and I tobogganed down Mount Everest. **_Whoopee!_'** She winked at them both. 'Now then, we should really fix that sleigh properly before you head off again, shouldn't we?'

'We should,' agreed Nick humbly. 'Shall I run back and fetch your tool kit, or . . . ?'

'No need, dearie. No need,' Granny told

him, tapping her nose. 'I've just had one of my brilliant wee ideas.'

They hurried back to the sleigh together, with Nick, Harry and some of the robot hands hauling the heavy sack of presents along between them. Once there, Granny jumped down from her amazing machine and *unscrewed* one of its robot arms. 'This should do the trick,' she said, lashing it firmly to the back of the sleigh with a string of twinkling fairy lights that she pulled from her pocket. 'A special **granny knot** will keep it all together, you'll see.' Her fingers tied and twisted until the robot arm was firmly in place, so that not a single present could escape. Then she stood back proudly to examine her work. 'There. Good enough for you to fly round the world and home again. I'll fix it properly when you get back – or maybe Harry can! He's very good with the tool kit these days.'

Nick hugged Granny. 'I can't thank you enough,' he said.

Harry hugged her too, feeling warm with pride at her words. 'You're the best,' he told her.

'**Och, all in a day's work!**' said Granny, patting them fondly. 'Now then – are you going to deliver these presents, or are you going to stand around chatting all night? Off you go, Father Christmas. *Second time lucky!*'

Nick climbed back into the sleigh and took the reins. '**UP!**' he commanded once more and, hooves glittering, the reindeer rose up off the ground. Then they kicked out their legs and the sleigh zoomed off again, up into the dark sky, with the fairy lights along the back sparkling almost as brightly as the stars. Harry waved and **waved**, smiling as he noticed how the big scoop of the SnowThrow arm seemed to wave right back at them.

Once the sleigh had vanished safely out of sight, Harry grinned at his granny. 'Well, your genius SnowThrow saved the day,' he said. Then he hesitated, looking rather bashful. 'I don't suppose . . . Do you think there might be room in that for both of us? I'd love to have a go.'

'**Absolutely!**' cried Granny, showing him how to clamber inside. Then she scrambled up beside him, pressed a button and together they strode through the snow, **CLANK CLANK.**

WHIRR, all the way home.

*

The following morning, Granny opened her eyes and smiled. She could hear the faint sound of elvish Christmas songs, bells ringing, and the squawk of a hungry penguin. It was **Christmas Day** – the best day of the year! And – wait a moment. There seemed to be something *very* heavy at the end of her bed. Surely she was too old to have had a visit from Father Christmas herself?!

Granny rubbed her eyes and stared at the large box with a bright red ribbon on top that had appeared there while she'd been asleep. Then she hopped out of bed, untied the ribbon and lifted the lid to see . . .

'**Oh! My engine!**' she cried happily. 'It's finally here!'

Hearing her voice, Nick popped his head around the door. 'Happy Christmas!' he said. 'I took a slight detour around the South Pole last night. Thought I'd drop in and collect your engine from the warehouse for you.'

'Goody gumdrops!' cheered Granny, dancing a little jig. 'Thank you very much.'

'**Thank** *you*,' said Nick. 'Thank you for fixing the sleigh last night and for collecting all those dropped presents . . . and for bringing a bit of sparkle to our lives too.' He laughed. 'By the way, those fairy lights on the sleigh were *so* useful when we ran into some fog around

London. From now on, I've decided that the Christmas sleigh will have fairy lights on it *every* year.'

'**Hooray!**' cried Granny, clapping her hands. Then she smiled as Percy waddled in to see her with a present in his beak. 'An icicle, how kind of you, darling,' she said, stroking his feathered head. 'And now I should get dressed. We've a *plane* to build, Percy!'

Later that morning, while the others took the SnowThrow off to a large empty field to enjoy the best ever Christmas morning snowball fight, Granny and Percy headed to Granny's workshop. After quite a lot of drilling, welding and hammering, the new plane was finished and looked fantastic.

The paint was fabulously shiny.

The seats were wonderfully comfortable.

And if you wanted a biscuit, cup of tea or smelly fish head, all you had to do was press a button and it was right there for you. **Yum!**

Before Granny and Percy said goodbye and headed off on another adventure, there was just time to give out some Christmas presents. A *beautiful* jumper for Nick. A *wonderful* new bed for Wolfie. And for Harry?

'I couldn't help noticing how much you enjoyed helping me in the workshop,' Granny told him. 'And how *good* you are at making machines yourself! So I'm leaving you the SnowThrow, to have some fun with. Change it around, add new features – do what you want with it. It's yours!'

'**Thank you!**' Harry said with a big grin.

There were some presents for Granny too, of course. Between them, Nick, Harry and the elves had made her a whole tin of yummy Christmas shortbread, a splendid new hat and a fluffy pair of slippers. They had also made a new waistcoat and water pistol for Percy which he was *very* chuffed about.

Then it was time for Granny and Percy to strap on their flying goggles and load up the plane.

'**Come and see us again soon!**' called Nick as Granny started the engine.

'Thanks for everything!' shouted Harry, waving as the little plane began to trundle along its runway. Then Granny flicked a lever, the engines roared and **WHOOSH!** the plane shot into the air, up into the bright blue sky. They just heard a faint shout – '**MERRY CHRISTMAS!** *Goodbye!*' –

carried down to them on the wind, and then Granny and Percy had gone.

Nick felt very happy. According to the Tinselnet, children all around the world were delighted with this year's Christmas presents. It had been a huge success!

Harry felt very happy. He couldn't wait to tinker about with the SnowThrow . . . he and the elves were going to have great fun with it!

As for Wolfie, he was *very* happy to have a brand-new bed with no penguin feathers or terrible smells. He was **so pleased**, in fact, that he decided to try it out, with a special Christmas nap. He curled up inside it, tucked his tail in around him and closed his eyes. Yes, it was extremely comfortable, he decided. And then . . . *ZZZzz* . . . he fell fast asleep.

THE END

A REAL
FAMILY
CHRISTMAS

CHAPTER ONE

Another year had flown by and it was already December again . . . but this Christmas was already shaping up to be quite different. For one thing, a postcard had arrived a few weeks earlier from a tiny island in the Indian Ocean. Home for Christmas! read the neat handwriting of Nick and Harry's mum. Can't wait to see you boys!

Both brothers were delighted

Hello boys!
Home for Christmas.
Can't wait to see
you both.
Love and hugs
Mum and Dad
xxx

AIR MAIL

Nick and Harry
NORTH POLE
the ARCTIC

at the thought of their parents' return. It had been three years now since their dad, **Nicholas Senior**, had retired from Father Christmas duties and handed on the responsibility to Nick. Since then, their mum and dad had been enjoying a *very* long holiday, travelling around the world and having lots of adventures. But Christmas was still a time for family, and it was going to be really special to have the four of them back together again to celebrate under the same roof. Even better, their parents might even lend a hand here and there in the run-up to the *Big Night*, thought Harry with a smile. They were Christmas experts, after all!

The postcard hadn't said exactly *when* Nicholas Senior and Angela would be arriving but Nick and Harry got everything ready anyway. They took time out from wrapping and labelling presents for all the good and kind children around the world to make sure that the spare room was clean and tidy, there were fresh sheets on the bed, and that there was plenty of food and drink in the house, all set for the **Big Day**.

'It'll be just like old times,' Harry said, remembering their happy family Christmases gone by.

And so, when there was a knock on the door one morning in the week before Christmas – **KNOCK-KNOCKITY-KNOCK** – the two brothers jumped up from the breakfast table at once.

'They're here!' cried Nick, hurrying into the hall. Harry rushed after him, beaming, and so did Wolfie, barking excitedly.

'**Hello!**' cried Nick and Harry in the same voice as Nick threw open the front door. Then they stopped and stared.

'*Oh*,' said Harry in surprise. Because the people standing there were definitely *not* his mum and dad.

'Uncle Rufus and Auntie Ruby!' said Nick, blinking. Then he remembered his manners. 'Er . . . **come in!**

Lovely to see you!' he added politely.

'**Dear boys!** We felt so *sorry* for you,' Auntie Ruby said, heaving a huge suitcase over the doorstep with a *THUMPITY-THUMP*. She clapped a hand to her chest with a sorrowful expression. 'It quite broke my heart to hear you would be on your own for Christmas, *again*. I said to Rufus, We can't have that! Didn't I, Rufus?'

'**Eh? What? Yes**,' said Uncle Rufus who was hauling in his own suitcase. Outside, it was snowing and a few stray snowflakes sparkled in his bushy moustache. 'Whatever you say, dear.'

Harry looked at Nick in confusion, and then back to the new arrivals. 'So you've . . . come to *stay*?' he guessed. 'For Christmas?'

'Well, yes, we couldn't exactly *leave* you, could we?' Auntie Ruby cried, stamping the snow off her boots and then peeling off gloves and a woolly hat. '**Not at Christmas!** Dear me, no. Christmas is for families being together. And so here we are!'

'Great,' Nick said. 'And actually Mum and Dad will be joining us too at some point, so we'll have a full house this year. The more the merrier!' he added, when Uncle Rufus and Auntie Ruby looked surprised to hear the news. 'Come on through, we were just having breakfast. Are you hungry? There's plenty for all of us.'

Nick and Harry busied themselves looking after their surprise guests. Nick made a fresh pot of tea while Harry fried eggs and bacon, and buttered toast. Wolfie helped by gulping down a piece of dropped bacon and then enthusiastically licked the floor where it had fallen, wagging his tail.

'**Ahhh!** That's better,' said Auntie Ruby leaning back in her chair after she'd eaten an enormous plateful. 'Now, I could do with a little nap after our long journey. How about you, Rufus?'

'Splendid idea,' he said. 'And after that . . . ' He wrestled to get something from his case . . . and eventually pulled out an **enormous** jigsaw. 'Aha! This will keep us all busy. Ten thousand pieces, this one. Super!'

Nick was making bedroom calculations.

They'd already set up the spare room for their parents, but perhaps his aunt and uncle could sleep there instead. Then if he moved his things into the tiny box room, he could prepare *his* room for his mum and dad. No problem. '**Follow me**,' he said.

Once Auntie Ruby and Uncle Rufus were settled in upstairs and Harry had washed up all the breakfast things, the two brothers got ready to leave for the day's work. The workshop was, of course, still **extremely** busy, with everyone needed to do their share of the present-making and wrapping.

Just as they were about to set off though, there came *another* knock on the door.

KNOCK-KNOCKITY-KNOCK!

'*This* must be Mum and Dad,' said Nick, hurrying to let them in, with Harry and Wolfie rushing along behind.

But when the door was open . . . Once again, the two brothers were surprised to see some unexpected faces there.

'**Will?**' said Nick, blinking.

'**Bill?**' said Harry, wide-eyed.

'*Phil!*' they both said, startled. 'What are you guys doing here?'

Will, Bill and Phil were their three wild cousins, all of them wearing party hats, Hawaiian shirts and baggy shorts, even though the snow was still billowing down.

'*Surprise!*' whooped Will, blowing a party tooter.

'**Merry Christmas!**' bellowed Bill, throwing streamers in the air.

'**The party starts here!**' cheered Phil, laughing as he flung his arms round Nick and Harry. '***Woo-hoo!***'

'Great,' said Nick, looking pleased but slightly bewildered. 'Good to see you all again. Come in! Are you . . . planning to stay?'

'Too right!' said Will. 'We heard you were on your own for Christmas. We couldn't have that!'

'No way,' agreed Bill. 'Don't worry, lads, we've brought the fun with us. This Christmas is going to be the *best*!'

Harry frowned. 'Why does everyone keep worrying about us being on our own?' he asked. 'We were fine last time when it was just the two of us.' In fact, he thought, apart from Nick being ill, it had been **much easier** when the two brothers had been alone than when Granny had come to stay!

Phil was already talking over him though. 'Hey, have you got any **food?**' he asked, dropping a large backpack in the hall. 'We are *starving*. We had to hitch-hike most of the way across the Arctic. Man, **you two are really cut off out here!**'

'We certainly are,' laughed Nick. 'And we've got plenty of food to share. This way!'

Once again, the two brothers got to work, looking after their new guests. Eggs, bacon, toast, coffee . . . Wolfie's nose twitched hopefully as delicious smells filled the air. The kitchen echoed with laughter too as Will, Bill and Phil told funny stories about what they'd been up to over the last few years.

Will had a job as a dancer on a cruise ship and he gave everyone a quick lesson on how to jive.

Bill worked as a clown on a children's hospital ward and told them lots of brilliant jokes.

And Phil was a magician who had his own TV show, and performed some amazing tricks around the table. Wolfie was astonished when Phil made his favourite squeaky bone disappear . . . only for it to reappear in the fridge.

'**It's so good to be here**,' said Will after a while, resting his hands on his full tummy. 'And I'm really glad you two won't be on your own. Christmas without a family get-together is all wrong. Right?'

'Wrong,' agreed Bill, draining his coffee cup. 'I mean, right. But don't worry, we're here now, so you won't have a chance to be lonely. *Or bored!*'

Nick and Harry exchanged a glance. 'Thanks,' said Nick. 'Although we're actually not on our own this year, funnily enough. Mum and Dad are coming to stay and Auntie Ruby and Uncle

Rufus have just arrived too, so . . . '

'Who told you we were alone anyway?' Harry wanted to know.

The three cousins looked at one another in surprise. 'Oh!' said Phil. 'It was –'

But just then there was *another* knock at the door. **KNOCK-KNOCKITY-KNOCK!** Except it was quite a faint, feeble sort of knock, so it sounded more like this: KNOCK-KNOCKITY-KNOCK!

'That must be Mum and Dad at last,' said Nick.

'**I hope so**,' said Harry in a low voice, following him out of the room. 'I don't know if we've got enough beds for any more visitors.'

Nick opened the door . . . but nobody was

there. Or rather, not a single *person* was there. Down on the doormat was a very tired-looking *pigeon*, with an envelope in its beak.

'For us?' Nick said. 'Thank you.'

'You look exhausted,' Harry added, seeing how droopy the pigeon's wings were. 'Would you like a piece of toast before you fly away again?'

The pigeon nodded gratefully and Harry bent down and held out a hand for

it to hop onto. Together they went back to the kitchen where Harry gave the pigeon a drink of water and a toast crust to peck at. Nick, meanwhile, was opening the letter.

'It's from Granny,' he said, then read it aloud.

'Dear boys, Percy and I are having a thrilling time in the jungle – what an adventure! By the way, I mentioned to a few other family members that they should pop in and spend Christmas with you if they are passing. I would hate you boys to be lonely! Love Granny.'

'I was just about to say, it was Granny who told us we should come here,' Phil explained.

'She told us you could do with the company, that she was **worried** about you being on your own,' Will added.

'Well, you're welcome to stay with us,' Nick said, frantically trying to think how he could squeeze everyone in. Auntie Ruby and Uncle Rufus were in the spare room. His mum and dad would have his bedroom. So if Harry camped out in the tiny box room with Nick, then Will, Phil and Bill could share Harry's room. It would be a bit of a **squash**, but they could manage, he decided. And it would be fun to have a big family Christmas for a change. 'The more the merrier!' he said again. **'Right, Harry?'**

Harry grinned, noticing that the pigeon had curled up in the tea cosy and fallen asleep. 'And the pigeon too,' he said. One thing was for sure: Christmas was definitely *not* going to be quiet this year!

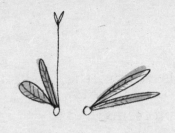

CHAPTER TWO

That evening, having worked all day in the Christmas workshop, Nick and Harry set about cooking dinner for their five guests. This was **way more complicated** than they'd thought.

Auntie Ruby was vegetarian.

Uncle Rufus didn't like olives, grapes, mushrooms, onions, carrots, fish or potatoes.

Will mostly ate salt and vinegar crisps.

Bill only liked food that was **brown**.

Phil wasn't fussy – but kept practising his

magic skills around the kitchen which caused their own problems.

'Where did I put that string of sausages?' Harry would wonder, only for Phil to cry *'Abracadabra!'* and make the sausages

appear in Wolfie's food bowl. This was not at *all* helpful – although Wolfie was delighted.

As for the pigeon, whenever anyone went near the toaster, its beady eyes lit up hungrily. 'Coo?' it would say hopefully, head cocked. **'Coo-*coo?*'**

They had just finished eating when there was a knock at the door: KNOCK-KNOCKITY-KNOCK!

Followed by a loud *'Yoohoo!* Are you there, boys?'

Nick smiled.

Harry laughed. *'Mum and Dad!'* they cried together, rushing to let their parents in.

It was *so nice* to see them again! Nick hugged Dad. Harry hugged Mum. Wolfie jumped up excitedly, trying to lick everyone's face all at once.

'Look how grown up and handsome you two are!' sighed Mum proudly. She looked tanned and healthy, and her bag *bulged* with exciting-looking presents.

'What a great job you've both been doing,' said Dad, just as proudly, propping up a rather battered surfboard against the grandfather clock.

And then – 'Goodness me, *hello,* **everyone**, this *is* jolly!' they both cried as they followed Nick and Harry into the kitchen and saw the others gathered there.

Nick laughed. 'It's going to be a fun family Christmas all right,' he said, 'although I'm glad that knock on the door was from you, and not anyone else,' he added in a low voice. 'It's a **full house!**'

'Coo,' agreed the pigeon, pecking

impatiently at the bread bin. '**_Coo!_**'

But just then – **guess what?** In the very next moment, there was _another_ knock at the front door. KNOCK-KNOCKITY-KNOCK!

Harry was starting to feel as if he was in a peculiar sort of dream as he went to answer it. Living where they did, right up near the North Pole, they hardly _ever_ had visitors. Their door knocker was so rarely used that he'd practically forgotten what it sounded like – until today, that was. Today, he was going to dream about that KNOCK-KNOCKITY-KNOCK all night!

He opened the door to see a very elderly man and a little girl there this time. The elderly man had white wispy hair and leaned on a stick. He was so tall and skinny that Harry half expected the wind to blow him over. And next to him was a small girl with plaited black hair, chocolate-brown eyes and a very sad face.

'**Hello, there**,' Harry said, wondering who these new arrivals might be. 'Come in, out of the cold. **Um** . . .'

'I'm your Great-Uncle Alf,' said the man as he tottered into the hallway. 'And this is Ivy, my great-niece. We're joining you for Christmas!'

'Lovely,' Harry replied politely, closing the front door. 'Hello, Ivy, how old are you? Let me guess . . . twenty-seven? Forty-two?'

He was trying to make her **smile** because she looked so serious but she just shook her head. 'Seven,' she said in a tiny voice, looking at the floor.

Just then Harry's mum came out and saw them there. 'Alf!' she cried, hugging him. 'And you must be Ivy. I heard your baby brother was a bit poorly, is that right? And Mummy and Daddy are staying in hospital with him? Well, you can have a lovely Christmas with us. **We'll look after you!** Won't we, Harry?'

'Absolutely,' said Harry. No wonder Ivy didn't look very happy. *Poor little thing!* 'Sorry to hear about your brother,' he said kindly to her.

Ivy was still staring at the floor. 'I just want to go home,' she whispered unhappily.

'I understand,' said Harry. 'Home is the best

place at Christmas, isn't it? But the next best place is here, I promise. I'm Harry, by the way and we must be distant cousins, I suppose. I'll **try my hardest** to make sure you have a really good Christmas. Deal?'

Ivy didn't move for a moment but then she nodded. Just a tiny nod, but it was enough.

'Great,' said Harry. 'Let's take these snowy boots off then, and I'll find you something yummy to eat. This way!'

*

The Christmas house had never *been* so full that night! After a bit of thought, a lot of camp-bed wrangling and much pillow-finding, Nick and Harry had finally made space for everyone.

Auntie Ruby and Uncle Rufus would be sleeping in the spare room.

Mum and Dad were in Nick's room.

Will, Bill and Phil were in Harry's room.

Great-Uncle Alf was in the tiny box room.

A bed had been made for Ivy up in the attic.

As for Nick and Harry, they were going to have to camp out on **sofas** in the living room. *Phew!* 'If anyone else arrives, we'll have to sleep in the workshop,' Nick said.

'Or bunk in with the elves!' Harry laughed.

(The pigeon, in case you were wondering, seemed very fond of sleeping in the tea cosy.)

That evening over dinner, they lit candles and sang songs together, and talked about funny family times. It felt really cosy, having so many people there together. But Ivy was still quiet, Harry noticed. She hardly cracked a smile when Will started doing a **crazy tango** with Auntie Ruby. She hadn't giggled once at Bill's jokes, even the really *silly* ones. And although Phil had done his best to astonish her with his **magic tricks**, she still looked mostly sad.

Poor Ivy! thought Harry as he got ready for bed later on. He felt more determined than ever to make sure her Christmas was a happy one. And he would start tomorrow, he decided, by taking her along to the workshop to meet the elves and see all the presents being made and wrapped. It was the **most exciting, wonderful place in the *world*,** after all: the heart of Christmas itself! Ivy couldn't fail to be cheered up there.

With that happy thought in mind, he rolled over, closed his eyes and fell fast asleep.

*

Meanwhile, up in the attic, Ivy was lying wide awake. There were lots of strange shadowy shapes around her from the piles of boxes and suitcases stored up there, and she kept hearing peculiar *creaks* and *groans* as the house settled down for the night. She sighed, wondering how her baby brother Robin was.

'I've got some **good news** for you,' Dad had told her, trying to sound cheerful. 'While Mum and I are in the hospital with Robin, Great-Uncle Alf has very kindly offered to take you all the way to the North Pole for Christmas. And guess where you're going to stay? With **Father Christmas** himself!'

Ivy hadn't wanted to go to the North Pole, not even to see Father Christmas. She wanted to be with her mum and dad, and with Robin too. Even though Harry had been kind to her, and everyone was very jolly, she was missing her own family too much to feel like joining in. She wished everything could go back to normal, and that they were all at home **together again**.

The old timbers of the house creaked once more and she sat up, feeling as if she would never be able to sleep. Gazing out of the sloping skylight, she could see the bright stars spangling the dark sky outside, and the great white pearl of the moon shining softly down across the snowy hills. Somewhere under that same moon were Mum, Dad and Robin, she thought, feeling very far away, and a tear trickled down her cheek. Without them, this was going to be the **worst Christmas *ever*!**

CHAPTER THREE

The following morning after breakfast, Nick,
Harry and Ivy headed out to the workshop. It was
quite a relief to get outside into the fresh cold air,
and enjoy some **peace and quiet** for a change!
Having a house full of guests was turning out to be
very hectic. There had been a long queue outside
the bathroom first thing. There were **grumbles**
about how cold it had been at night. Uncle
Rufus couldn't find his glasses and Great-Uncle
Alf had lost one of his slippers. And, of course,
everyone wanted different things for breakfast.

Even the pigeon was **bossily** demanding extra toast and pecking the toaster for not being fast enough. 'Coo,' it said, impatiently. '**Coo-*coo!***' (Wolfie gave a deep doggy sigh when he saw this. Just what they needed: another annoying bird in the house. Hadn't the penguin been bad enough last year?)

Outside, the snow was falling so thickly that it was hard to see where you were going. But the lights of the workshop were **shining brightly** ahead of them, and even from a distance you could hear the sound of elvish laughter and singing coming from the building. Ivy breathed in the scents of ginger and cinnamon and vanilla wafting out through an open window, and felt a bit *tingly* with excitement all of a sudden.

She was actually going to see the Christmas workshop and meet some real elves. Wait until she told her friends at school about *this*!

'Here we are,' said Nick as they reached the entrance. He pushed open the big workshop door. '**Come on in**.'

Ivy stepped into the warm, busy workshop, her eyes wide as she tried to take everything in. There were elves *everywhere*, making wooden toys, cuddly toys, electronic toys, sporty toys, arty toys and hundreds more. There were elves baking ginger biscuits and shaping colourful lollipops. There were elves testing out funny little robots, and Frisbees, and train sets. There were elves wrapping presents, with great rolls of paper and glittering spools of ribbon . . .

'**Wow**,' breathed Ivy, gazing around in wonder.

Harry smiled at the look on her face then called out to the elves. 'Guys! This is Ivy!'

Instantly the workshop fell silent as the elves turned around, and then, a split-second later, they were all rushing over to meet her.

'A girl! **A *real* human girl!**' they cried excitedly, beaming and crowding about her. 'Hello, Ivy. **Welcome!**'

'I'm Cherry!' said one with red curly hair.

'I'm Biff,' said one with a silver beard and twinkly eyes.

'I'm Eve!' 'I'm Pip!' 'I'm Ribbons!' 'I'm Holly!' other elves said, pressing in around her.

'Okay, one at a time!' Nick laughed. 'We

don't get many visitors here, as you can imagine,'
he said to Ivy. 'That makes you very **special**.'

'Tell me, Ivy, what do you think of this
teddy?' the elf called Ribbons asked in the next
moment, holding up a plush brown bear with a
smiley face. 'Is it *cuddly* enough?'

'Ooh! And what do you think of this doll?'

asked another elf – Holly, was it? – holding up a doll with yellow hair in a pink dress. 'Does she look *friendly* enough to you?'

'How about these cookies?' asked an elf with flour on the end of her nose and tinsel around the ends of her plaits. She held out a plate of tasty-looking cookies. 'Do you think they need more nutmeg, perhaps? Some extra *cinnamon?*'

'**Whoa**, **whoa**, don't overwhelm her,' cried Harry, but Ivy couldn't help smiling back at all the eager elves.

'I don't mind helping,' she said shyly, giving the teddy a cuddle. 'Perfect,' she said to Ribbons. 'The doll is really nice,' she added politely to Holly. Then she nibbled the cookie which tasted absolutely delicious. 'That is so good!' she said, taking another bite almost immediately. 'Really yummy!'

Nick and Harry needed to get on with their work but Ivy was soon having **a lovely time** with the elves. She cuddled a *lot* of teddies, pandas, bunnies and lions. She tested out some very cool roller skates with flashing lights, and Jingle taught her how to do spins which was really fun. Then she played several board games with Rudy and Biff, tested lollies in the elf kitchen (pineapple was her favourite flavour) and tried on all sorts of dressing-up clothes to make sure they were a good fit.

She was having **such** a great time, in fact, that it wasn't until Perky and Eve showed her the baby toys that she suddenly remembered

Robin and went a bit quiet. '. . . And these are the new rattles we've designed which are . . .' Eve was saying, until she saw the sad look on Ivy's face. '**Oh. Is everything all right?**' she asked in concern.

There was a lump in Ivy's throat suddenly. 'I've got a baby brother,' she replied. 'But he's not very well.' Tears brimmed in her eyes as she thought about him. Robin was only tiny but he had already learned how to smile and he especially loved it when Ivy made funny faces at him. He would gurgle with laughter sometimes and it was such a cute sound that everyone else always joined in. It felt **all wrong** that Ivy wouldn't get to make Robin smile and laugh on Christmas Day.

Eve's green eyes were full of sympathy and she put an arm round Ivy. 'I'm **sorry** to hear that,' she said. 'That must be tough.'

'I've had an idea!' said Perky. 'Why don't you choose a present for him? We'll wrap it and label it for your baby brother so that Father Christmas knows where to deliver it on Christmas Eve.'

Ivy's eyes went very round. 'Does Father Christmas deliver presents to babies too?' she asked. 'Even if they're in hospital?'

'**Of course he does!**' Eve cried. 'He likes to give extra-nice treats to little ones in hospital. Perky, that's a great idea. What do you say, Ivy? Do you want to choose something *really special* for your brother?'

'Yes please,' Ivy said at once. She smiled,

feeling glad that she could do something nice for Robin. '**Thank you!**'

'No problem,' said Perky, looking pleased with himself. 'What do you think he might like?'

Ivy and the elves began looking through all the lovely toys and gifts that had been made especially for babies. **It was hard to choose!** A small cuddly elephant? A shaker with brightly coloured beads inside? A chewy teething ring for when Robin's gums were sore? After a few minutes, Ivy finally decided on a pale blue teddy with little heart shapes stitched into the ends of his paws. 'I think he would like this, please,' she said.

'Good choice!' said Perky with a grin.

'I made that one. Now then, come and choose the wrapping paper, and we'll get this safely into the present sack for you.'

Ivy followed him over to the wrapping station, where she picked out some midnight-blue paper and a *sparkly* silver ribbon. Then, as Perky deftly wrapped the bear, a thought popped into her head. Wait a minute – if Father Christmas would be visiting the hospital where Robin was staying, and delivering his present there . . . maybe Ivy could hop in the sleigh and go too. That way she would still see her family!

'Um . . . Perky, does Father Christmas ever let **anyone else** go on his sleigh with him?' she asked, trying to keep the excitement out of her voice.

'No,' said Perky, addressing a silver star-shaped gift tag. 'It's just Father Christmas and the reindeer on the **Big Night**. With all the presents he has to deliver, there's no room for anyone else.'

Ivy felt disappointed . . . but not for long. Her mind was racing. If she could maybe hide herself away on the sleigh without Nick realising she was there, she could *jump out* when they reached the hospital and see her family. Her heart pounded as she imagined the scene. Mum's surprised face. Dad giving her one of his big squeezy hugs. And Robin giggling and gurgling as Ivy bent over his cot with her gift!

Following Perky as he took her to put the

beautifully wrapped present in a big brown sack, Ivy made up her mind. **Yes**. Somehow or other, she was going to get herself **into that sleigh on Christmas Eve**. She had to!

CHAPTER FOUR

Over the next few days, Nick and Harry worked **very hard** to get all the last-minute Christmas presents and preparations finished. But as well as that, they had everyone to look after, the house to keep clean and the food cupboards to keep full. Unfortunately, their guests *did not* make things easy!

Great-Uncle Alf liked watching old films on television with the sound up so loud that nobody else could hear themselves speak.

Uncle Rufus had set out his very big jigsaw

puzzle on the dining-room table but got very bossy if anyone tried to help him. 'It's *my* jigsaw and **I make the rules**,' he kept saying. 'Edge pieces first and that's that!'

Will and Phil had had an extremely messy food fight in the kitchen – and Auntie Ruby, who happened to walk in right in the middle of it, had *not* appreciated being ***covered***, head to toe, in icing sugar.

Bill had been practising his clown tricks, juggling oranges while whizzing around on his skateboard. But he'd been startled by a large '**COO!**' from the pigeon, and accidentally sent one of the oranges hurtling towards Uncle Rufus's jigsaw table. ***BASH!*** went the orange, sending a whole corner of the jigsaw flying in pieces to the carpet. 'Now look what you've done!' grumbled Uncle Rufus.

As for Nick and Harry's parents – well, they were helping out quite a lot, thank goodness. Nicholas Senior was doing **endless** washing-up while Angela was stocking up on the groceries and baking bread and Christmas cakes. The only small problem was that they were so delighted to see the elves again, they spent hours over at the workshop **chatting** and catching up on all the elvish news. Although this was nice for everyone, it did mean that the elves weren't getting very much work done.

The only person who *wasn't* any trouble was Ivy, thought Harry. She was still quiet and thoughtful, but seemed to enjoy being at the Christmas house a lot more now. She particularly liked going to visit the reindeer and getting to know them all. And she'd really loved seeing the sleigh too. In fact, she'd spent **ages** in the sleigh shed, as Harry showed her the special compartment to load in extra present sacks and where Father Christmas always sat.

'Can I see the reindeer and sleigh whenever I want to?' she had asked afterwards.

'**Of course!**' cried Harry, feeling pleased that she had taken such an interest. She really was a nice girl, he thought – far more interested in learning about Father Christmas's work than greedily listing all the presents she wanted for herself. 'I'll leave the shed door unlocked so you can pop in and out as you please,' he told her with a smile.

And then it was Christmas Eve, and everyone was feeling very excited about the **Big Night**.

Will was wearing his snazziest catsuit.

Uncle Rufus had trimmed his beard into the shape of a Christmas tree.

Great-Uncle Alf sang carols at the top of his voice and Phil was working on a magic trick where gold and silver parcels appeared from out of nowhere on people's lunch plates.

Bill kept telling festive jokes – 'What do you get if you cross Father Christmas with a duck? **A Christmas** *quacker!*' while Auntie Ruby made a fresh batch of mince pies.

As for Nick and Harry's parents, they tramped out to the forest and came back with **heaps** of holly, mistletoe and ivy, as well as a basket of logs to get a roaring Christmas fire going.

More importantly, it was almost time for Father Christmas to begin his magical journey! Harry asked Ivy to help him smear the glittering golden magic dust onto the reindeer hooves, the elves began carrying the heavy sacks stuffed full of presents out to the sleigh and Nick went to change into his **special** red and white Father Christmas outfit. Another wonderful Christmas was on its way, thought Harry happily. *Hooray!*

But in the very next minute, the trouble started.

Will had invented a new Christmas dance

and was demonstrating it to everyone, twirling around the kitchen and clapping his hands above his head. Unfortunately, as he twirled and whirled, he bumped into Auntie Ruby, who was getting her mince pies out of the oven.

BUMP! went Will.

'Yikes!' went Auntie Ruby.

The mince pies went flying – *WHEEEEE!* –

and one landed SPLAT on Uncle

Rufus's head.

'Ooh! Ah! Ooh!'

cried Uncle Rufus, jumping

up in alarm as hot mincemeat

and pastry trickled down his face.

He accidentally trod

on Bill's skateboard –

WHOOAAAAA! – and went **skidding** into the living room on it, arms flailing.

Great-Uncle Alf had been snoozing in an armchair and woke up with a start to see Uncle Rufus sailing towards him. 'Help! A burglar!' yelled Great-Uncle Alf, swinging his walking stick around in alarm.

Phil, who had been practising a trick where he swept the tablecloth off the table, leaving all the plates and glasses and cutlery there, was whacked by Great-Uncle Alf's stick and knocked the whole table over instead.

cRASH! sMASH! TINKLE!

went all the crockery and glasses, shattering into tiny pieces.

Meanwhile Angela and Nicholas Senior were on step-ladders, arranging trails of holly and ivy on the enormous Christmas tree. 'WAAAAAHHHH!' yelled Uncle Rufus as he whizzed straight towards them on the skateboard.

BANG! Down toppled Angela's ladder, sending her flying into the sofa. 'Eek!' she squeaked.

BANG! Down toppled Nicholas Senior's ladder, sending him flying onto the other sofa. 'Oof!' he grunted.

And then . . . *FLUMP!* Down fell the Christmas tree, plunging straight into the roaring log fire. Uncle Rufus just managed to scramble away before there was an enormous **WHOOMPH!** and the tree went up in flames.

WOOF! WOOF! WOOF! went Wolfie urgently, barking a warning.

'**COO!**' squawked the pigeon, falling off the curtain rail in surprise.

'**Fire!**' yelled Phil in alarm. 'Everyone get water!'

Then there was absolute chaos as all of them went charging to the sink to get bowls of water to throw on the flames. Bill and Will dashed outside to scoop up armfuls of snow in the hope of putting out the fire with that too.

Over in the sleigh shed, Harry and Ivy heard Wolfie's barks. 'What on earth . . . ?' said Harry in alarm. He had just finished putting dust on the last reindeer's hoof and jumped to his feet, peering out at the house. Even from that distance he could see the blazing Christmas tree through the window. '**Whoa!** Stay there, Ivy,' he ordered, sprinting over to try and help the others.

Back in the house, Nick was coming downstairs in his special red and white suit and gasped to see that the flames had spread right along the Christmas tree and were just starting to lick at the curtains. '**Oh my goodness**,' he cried in horror, grabbing one of the sofa cushions and beating back the flames with it.

Rushing in, Harry grabbed another big sofa cushion while the others dumped water and snow on the flames. Finally, with one last smoky *sizzle*, the fire went out.

The room became very quiet as everyone gazed around at the ruined Christmas tree and the scorched carpet and furniture. There was broken glass and china all over the floor and the table was still upended.

'What happened?' asked Harry, hardly able to take in the scene of devastation.

'I'm so sorry,' said Will, who had gone very pale. 'I was **dancing** . . .'

'And my mince pies went flying . . .' said Auntie Ruby, who had smuts on her cheeks.

'And I trod on a skateboard . . .' said Uncle Rufus, who still had pastry and mincemeat trickling down his face.

'It was my skateboard,' said Bill unhappily.

'**I thought it was a *burglar!***' said Great-Uncle Alf.

'My trick went wrong,' said Phil.

'And we'd just lit the fire . . .' said Mum and Dad.

'We're really sorry,' they all said

together in the next moment.

Nick and Harry looked at each other, unable to speak for a moment. They both felt *exhausted*. Weren't big family Christmases meant to be fun? Because this did not feel like a fun Christmas any more. The whole house could have burned down!.

Auntie Ruby was first to break the silence. **'We haven't been very good house guests, have we?'** she said apologetically.

'You boys have worked so hard and we've ruined everything,' fretted their mum.

'But we'll put it all right again,' promised Bill.

'Of course we will,' said Uncle Rufus.

'Don't give it another thought, Nick, we know you need to get going now,' said

Nicholas Senior. 'Leave this mess with us.'

'**And I'll get that *burglar!*'** shouted Great-Uncle Alf, still waving his stick.

Nick and Harry left the others explaining to him that there hadn't actually *been* a burglar, and tramped rather glumly outside to the sleigh. Nick tried to find his Christmas spirit again, reminding himself that the presents had been loaded on board the sleigh, and the reindeer were harnessed up and waiting, their hooves glimmering with magic. The stars were twinkling brightly in the dark sky above them and the elves were all waiting in a crowd to see them off, as usual. Christmas would still be okay. ***Wouldn't it?***

'Don't worry, I'll make sure all of this

gets sorted out,' Harry said tiredly as Nick climbed aboard the sleigh. 'You just have a great night. We've got some **brilliant** presents and all the children out there are going to be so happy and excited on Christmas morning. That's what matters, right?'

'Right,' agreed Nick. 'Thanks, Harry. I'll see you tomorrow.' The two brothers high-fived each other and Nick took a tight hold of the reins. '**UP!**' he commanded the reindeer.

There was a glittering swirl of magic as the reindeer kicked out their strong legs and then, in the next moment, they were galloping high up into the air, with the sleigh flying out behind them.

'*Goodbye!*' called the elves from down

below, waving excitedly. 'Good luck!'

Harry waved too, staring up at the sky until the very last gleam of light from the sleigh had vanished, then he glanced back towards the house. Will, Bill and Phil were dragging the burnt Christmas tree out through the front door. Auntie Ruby was flinging open the windows to let the smoke escape. He could see his dad in the kitchen getting the dustpan and brush. There was his mum too, filling a bucket with water.

Ivy! he thought suddenly. He had forgotten all about her in the mayhem. 'We should get you ready for bed soon, Ivy,' he said, turning back to the crowd of elves and trying to find her there. 'More importantly – we need to hang up your stocking!' He waited for a response but none came. He couldn't see her anywhere. 'Ivy?' he asked, searching for her face. **'Are you there?'**

The elves looked around too but nobody could see her. 'Ivy?' Harry shouted, starting to feel worried. She hadn't wandered off in the dark, had she? He glanced back at the house again but no light was on in the attic window. 'Ivy, *where are you?*'

'I'll check the workshop,' said Biff, hurrying over there with Elvis and Ginger.

'I'll check the shed,' said Cinnamon, racing off with Juniper and Peppermint.

'I'll check the house,' said Candy, sprinting away with Holly and Ribbons.

Meanwhile, Perky and Eve had been

whispering worriedly to one another nearby. After a moment, they approached Harry. 'Um . . . I think I might know where Ivy is,' Perky said, hanging his head.

'She was asking us if Father Christmas delivered presents to **babies in hospital**,' said Eve. 'She really misses her family, you see.'

'And then she asked if Father Christmas ever let anyone else go in the sleigh with him,' Perky went on. '**I said no**, but now I'm wondering . . . You don't think she would have sneaked on board anyway, do you?'

Biff came running back just then. 'She's not in the workshop,' he said.

Cinnamon came running back too. 'She's

not in the shed,' she said.

Candy came running back as well. 'She's not in the house,' she said.

Harry gazed up at the black sky where the sleigh was long gone. His mind was whirling. This was an absolute Christmas *disaster!*

CHAPTER FIVE

Miles from the Christmas house, Nick was just guiding the sleigh down onto a rooftop to make his first deliveries of the night. Having landed safely, he checked his list.

'Let's see: Kate, who loves football and Alex, who loves drawing,' he murmured to himself, reaching around to open the big sack of presents. He plunged his hand in to find their gifts and nearly fell off the sleigh when there was an unexpected rustling sound and then a **head** popped out of the sack.

239

'**Hello**,' said Ivy, who had been hiding there. She had dived into the sack after Harry had gone to help put out the fire and had been sitting very still and quietly until the sleigh took off. She couldn't help a smile of glee now. **Her plan had worked!** She was going around the world with Father Christmas on his Christmas Eve deliveries, and she'd get to see Mum, Dad and Robin too!

Nick's mouth fell open in surprise. 'Ivy! You're . . . you're not supposed to be here,' he gulped. '**Oh dear**. How has this happened?' He took off his furry hat and wiped his brow, shaking his head. 'We'll have to go home and drop you off, I'm afraid. I've got so much work to do tonight, I really can't –'

'**Oh please, *no!***' cried Ivy desperately. 'Please! I just want to see Robin, and my mum and dad.' Her chin started to wobble; she was trying very hard not to cry. Surely the plan couldn't go wrong now? '**I miss them so much!**'

Nick looked at her for a long moment then nodded slowly. 'Of course you do,' he said. 'I understand. Being with your family is what Christmas is all about – even if they *do* almost burn your house down.' He pulled a funny face.

'Well,' he went on thoughtfully, 'I could do with a **helper** tonight, since you're here. Do you think you can manage that?'

Ivy beamed. 'Yes,' she assured him. 'Oh yes, please!'

*

Back at the North Pole, the Christmas house was slowly being returned to normal. The broken glass and crockery had been swept up, the carpet had been cleaned, and the pong of burning was no longer quite so pungent. The dropped mince pies had all been cleared up (or eaten by a *delighted* Wolfie) and the floor gleamed where it had been mopped. Bill, Will and Phil had promised to go out and cut down a new Christmas tree from the forest in the morning, and everyone else had vowed to make some decorations for it. The pigeon, whose feathers had become quite ruffled with all the drama, had been given an extra piece of toast and was now asleep in the tea cosy again.

'We'll still have a **wonderful** Christmas,' Angela said bracingly as Harry trudged back into the house. 'And from now on, we'll all be working together.'

'One big family team,' agreed Uncle Rufus. 'I don't even mind if other people help with the jigsaw!' he added generously.

Harry was too worried to smile. '**Ivy's gone**,' he said flatly.

The others stared at him. 'What?' gasped Auntie Ruby.

'Gone where?' asked Phil in alarm.

'We think she might have **stowed away** on the sleigh, hoping to see her brother,' Harry said, sinking into the nearest chair with a groan. 'What if she falls out, or hurts herself? She might slip off a rooftop, or down a chimney. She might accidentally wake up other sleeping children and spoil the Christmas magic . . .' He put his head in his hands. **'I can't bear to think about it**.'

'Oh dear,' said Nicholas Senior. 'This is our fault too. If we hadn't caused so much trouble, you wouldn't have had to rush in and sort us out.'

Will was too dismayed even to dance.
'We've totally wrecked Christmas!'
he cried miserably.

*

Christmas, a wreck? Not as far as Ivy was concerned. She was having the most brilliant time with Father Christmas! It was so exciting to go skimming through the cold night air with the reindeer, seeing all the towns and cities lit up below. She was getting good at finding the right presents for each house and handing them over to Nick, and then sang Christmas songs to entertain the reindeer while he went inside to deliver them.

245

The closer they got to the hospital where Robin was, the **bigger** her smile became.

At last, they landed on the roof of the hospital and Nick winked at her. 'Here we are,' he said and consulted his list. 'Okay, there are quite a few children staying here tonight,' he went on, reading the names out while Ivy found each person's present '. . . and *Robin Christmas*,' he finished. 'I'm guessing we're both going to deliver the presents this time, right?'

Ivy's eyes shone with excitement as she pulled out the midnight-blue parcel tied with sparkly silver ribbon. The present she'd chosen for her brother. '**Yes,** *please!*' she said happily.

Once inside the hospital, Ivy and Father Christmas tiptoed through the wards of sleeping children, leaving presents for each of them. The nurses and doctors had made the place look as festive as possible with party streamers and bunting, and there was even a big tree with shiny baubles.

Down the corridors they crept towards the unit where babies were looked after. Nearly there! But then they heard a voice.

'**Nick?** I mean – *Father Christmas?* Is that *you?*'

Ivy spun around in alarm. Oh dear! A doctor was looking at them very sternly. They weren't about to be sent away, were they? Would she tell them off for being here?

But Nick was smiling and went over to hug the doctor. '**Annie!** Hello, there. Meet my new assistant, **Ivy**. We're looking for Robin, by the way. Robin Christmas? Ivy's little brother. She's got a special present for him.'

The doctor – Annie – smiled too and her eyes went all twinkly. *'Lucky Robin!'* she said. 'He's right this way. Follow me.'

Annie opened the door to the baby unit. It was dimly lit inside and you could hear the gentle bleep of machines. Long curtains hung from the ceiling down to the floor along the sides of the room, sectioning off the babies' cots. Beckoning them to follow her, Annie tiptoed through the ward until she reached some long red curtains. She quietly pulled them aside and Ivy gave an **excited squeak** as she saw Robin fast asleep in a cot there, and her mum and dad dozing in chairs by his side.

At the sound of the squeak, Ivy's mum opened her eyes and stared. 'Ivy!' she gasped. 'Is that you?'

Ivy was so happy, she couldn't speak all of a sudden. She flung herself into her mum's arms and hugged her tightly instead. 'Oh, my darling,' said her mum in astonishment. '**Am I dreaming?**'

'Happy Christmas,' whispered Nick, popping his head around the curtain. 'No, it's not a dream. Ivy's been helping me on my Christmas rounds. She was very keen to say hello.'

Ivy's mum beamed down at Ivy as if she couldn't believe her eyes. Then she elbowed her husband. '**Wake up! Look who's *here*!**' she said.

While Nick left them to finish his hospital deliveries, Ivy was hugged and kissed again and again by both her mum and dad. 'Fancy you being here with Father Christmas!' they exclaimed in delight. 'This is the best Christmas surprise ever. **We missed you *so* much!**'

'I missed you too,' she replied. 'And ***Robin***, of course.' She gently placed her present for him at the end of his cot and then a lovely thing happened. Robin's eyes opened and he blinked a few times. When he saw Ivy leaning over to peep at him, a huge smile appeared on his face. He gurgled happily. Then he **laughed!**

'He's looking so much better,' said Doctor Annie, checking Robin's temperature. 'What a big smile for your sister, young man!'

Just then, Nick came back in again, checking his watch. 'We'd better go, Ivy. Lots more deliveries to make before the sun comes up!'

Ivy hugged her mum and dad goodbye, and gently tickled Robin's feet. 'I'm glad I got to see you,' she said, feeling much happier.

'Us too,' her mum said, with a last kiss.

'**Safe journey** now, poppet.'

'And ***merry Christmas!*** added her dad.

*

Then they were off once more, flying through the air, stopping on rooftop after rooftop, delivering present after present. When Ivy felt too tired to help any more, Nick made up a cosy little bed for her in the back of the sleigh, and she dozed off until at last, with a ***THUMPETY-BUMP-BUMP***, it was the morning, and they had arrived back at the Christmas house.

Harry had waited up for them and sighed with relief when he saw Nick carrying in the sleeping Ivy. '**Oh, thank goodness!** I was so worried,' he said. He clapped Nick on the back. 'Well done. I'll take the reindeer to the stable and give them something to eat.'

Nick tucked Ivy into her bed and then took the very last present out of his sack and put it in her stocking. *There!* All his Christmas gifts had been delivered at last.

Then, feeling very tired, he and Harry both crawled into their sleeping bags and fell fast asleep.

*

A few hours later, Nick and Harry awoke to see the living room looking quite different. Everything was **spotlessly clean** and there was a new Christmas tree standing in the corner, festooned with beautiful hand-made decorations and iced gingerbread stars. In the kitchen, Will, Bill and Phil had made blueberry pancakes for everyone's breakfast, while Great-Uncle Alf squeezed oranges to make juice. Auntie Ruby and Uncle Rufus were in charge of tea and coffee-making, Angela was setting the table and Nicholas Senior had just come back from taking Wolfie for a lovely long walk. Ivy, meanwhile, was twirling around on a brand-new pair of **roller skates** that had really *cool flashing lights*.

'Thank you for my present!' she said delightedly as Nick came in. '**I love them!**'

'You are very welcome,' laughed Nick, ruffling her hair.

'*COO!*' said the pigeon with a very strange expression on its face. Then it stood up proudly to show everyone the egg it had just laid in the tea cosy.

'Oh, **good work!**' said Harry. He had grown very fond of the pigeon since it had come to stay. 'I suppose you'll be wanting some more toast now, will you?'

'**Coo-*coo*,**' the pigeon said approvingly, sitting back on its egg and looking very pleased with itself.

They were just settling down for their Christmas breakfast when Wolfie's ears pricked up at a sound from outside. **CHOP-CHOP-*CHOP*-CHOP-*CHOP*!**

'Goodness gracious, it's a helicopter!' said Uncle Rufus in surprise.

'It's Annie!' cried Harry, peering out of the window.

Ivy did a double spin of excitement on her roller skates and let out a *squeal* when she saw who else was in the helicopter. '**And my mum and dad!**' she cheered, her eyes wide. She waved at them and skated as fast as she could to the front door. 'And **Robin's there too –** he must be all better!'

The most enormous fuss was made of Ivy's mum and dad as they came in, and Robin too, who was pink in the cheeks and gurgling excitedly, especially when he saw Ivy. Then there were three cheers for Annie the doctor for bringing everyone together for a real family Christmas.

Nick and Harry looked at all their guests sitting around the breakfast table and felt **very** *very* happy and **very** *very* lucky. It was Christmas Day – the **best day** of the year! – and they were going to have such a lovely time together. *'Happy Christmas!'* said Nick, raising his cup of coffee in the air.

'HAPPY CHRISTMAS!' echoed everyone in return.

And do you know what? It really really was.

THE END